Praise for Piper Huguley

"Keep your eye on her. She's going to be a star!"
—*New York Times* bestselling author Beverly Jenkins

Look for these titles by Piper Huguley

Now Available:

Migrations of the Heart
A Virtuous Ruby

Coming Soon:

Migrations of the Heart
A Treasure of Gold

A Most Precious Pearl

Piper Huguley

Samhain Publishing, Ltd.
11821 Mason Montgomery Road, 4B
Cincinnati, OH 45249
www.samhainpublishing.com

A Most Precious Pearl

Print ISBN: 978-1-61923-146-7
Digital ISBN: 978-1-61922-742-2

Editing by Latoya Smith
Cover by Kanaxa

First Samhain Publishing, Ltd. electronic publication: September 2015
First Samhain Publishing, Ltd. print publication: September 2015

Dedication

To all young women who believe themselves to be ugly ducklings. Know that you are a swan in one way or another. Believe in yourself and you will fly.

Acknowledgements

Thank you so very much to all of my readers who continue to believe in these stories. Please know that your support means a great deal to me.

I would like to single out two forces in the publishing industry. Latoya Smith, thank you so much for taking me on. Thank you to Jessica Schmeidler, who wanted to. You ladies represent true vision in the publishing romance, where everyone is entitled to their Happily Ever After. Thank you so much for working to this worthwhile end.

Chapter One

Pittsburgh, Pennsylvania - 1919

"Get up and walk, Asa!"

His jaw clenched at the way the crucified Jesus on the brown wooden cross mocked him from across his bedroom.

How was he supposed to walk with a shot-off leg? Well, part of one anyway.

Life had no point. Yes, the great Asa Thomas Caldwell, intrepid, far-traveling Negro journalist for the *Pittsburgh Courier*, could only lay around in his mother's house—a cripple. That was the story. A sad one. If he had known about all of the pain and humiliation he would have to endure as Negro in The Great War, only to be treated like a criminal and have his leg shot off, he would never have gone to Europe. Not even for the big story.

Fluffy, white snowflake doilies decorated every surface in the room. His blood splatter would dirty some of them once he did it. His mother's gnarled brown fingers had shaped and made hundreds of those things.

His mother had felt such relief weeks ago. The redness in the corners of her brown eyes eased as she came to understand he had sustained an injury that meant he was not dead. Still, she would be mighty unhappy to see his blood on her doilies.

But he was a dead man—not even walking anyway.

There was no life this way. No dignity. No story here, folks.

This was the story. The end. His end. A small frisson of excitement, one he hadn't felt in weeks tickled his fingers as he touched the gun in his lap. Contraband. So what if he stole it? Since the white officer who shot off his leg didn't finish the job, he would do it. If he could get through all of the humiliation of The Great War, he could muster the strength to get it over with. He tried to care that his mother would have to find him in here, bleeding onto her clean white sheets, with his iron-rich blood splatter on her snowy white doilies, but he couldn't live this way anymore. How could anyone who loved him expect him to live a life without dignity?

He picked up the gun and his hand sagged at the heavy weight of it. He stroked the top part of the pistol, ready to pull the trigger back, but he kept on running his thumb over it, rather than cocking it. Something was staying his hand but he didn't know what.

His mother's footsteps echoed down the hallway. A knock sounded on the door and he scrambled as much as he could. He didn't want her to see him with the gun, but he couldn't reach over quickly enough to put it away in the drawer where he kept it. He took up a towel and covered it.

"Asa? You have a visitor, son."

"I don't want any visitors. I'm resting."

Shuffles in the hallway. Who could the visitor be? He moved a little lower down into the covers, taking the posture like he was going to sleep, but he took care of where the gun was on his lap. He didn't want to do anything stupid, like miss or sustain some other injury like he already had. The door opened, without knocking.

"Mother," he made his voice firm to discourage her, but with his mother, stood an ethereal vision. "Sister Ruby, what are you doing here?"

Ruby stayed his mother's hand and she came farther into the room, right next to his bedside. It was as if a bright beam of light had entered his heavy mind and imaginings. She was a beautiful cream-colored Negro woman with lots of silky, jet-black hair and lively brown eyes. Her rounded belly, full of her husband's child, reminded him of the burgeoning promise of life, and seemed to be an impossibility in this dark and hopeless world they lived in. Before the war, Ruby gave him what he thought was admiring glances in the church, but now, she fixed him with a critical piercing gaze. "Wondering what someone like you is doing hiding yourself away from the world like this."

He usually thrilled to her soft Southern drawl. However, Ruby was madly and completely in love with her husband, Dr. Adam Morson. The slight crush he had on her would result in nothing. Yet another reason to feel hopeless. No woman would ever want him this way. He turned his face away from her. "You shouldn't be in a man's bedroom. You should be at home getting ready for your baby or something."

Ruby raised a hand. "I'm a nurse. You forget, I've seen it all. I'm not intimidated by you."

Something caused him to turn his head. "What do you want?"

"I need your help."

Help? Sister Ruby? Something inside of him shifted. "I can't do anything for anyone. My left leg is gone."

"Part of your left leg is gone. There is still plenty of work for you to do if you will do it, instead of staying cooped up in here, driving your mother and sisters crazy trying to make you happy."

She stepped over to his bed, coming closer, a bright light in her white house dress that barely hid her rounded belly. A glow, maybe generated by her child, fairly radiated off of her. He didn't need to see her light and wanted no part of it. She reached behind him and pulled out pillows from behind his head, forcing him to shift position and inadvertently, he grabbed at the gun, pulling it out. She kept fluffing and adjusting his pillows. "Sit up."

When she finished, she held out a small slim hand for the gun and directed a steel-driven form of her Southern drawl to him, "Give it to me."

"No."

"Then I'll tell your mother. It's military issue, isn't it? You could go to jail for having it."

"I don't care."

"Give it to me. Now."

He had a small measure of sympathy for her four-year old son, Solomon. If his mother spoke to him like this when he misbehaved, it was no wonder he was one of the best behaved little children in their church.

"You shouldn't be handling a gun. You, you're going to have a baby."

"I'm a country girl. I know all about guns. Give it here."

He reluctantly obeyed and Ruby took the gun across the room and put it on a bookshelf. "There. If you want it, you'll have to get it yourself."

"That's not fair."

"It's not fair for you stay up in here, thinking you have the right to take what gifts God has given you and throw them away," Ruby's brown eyes turned into inflamed coals. "I need your help. Get up from this bed." She picked up a carved wooden cane and threw it at his head.

"Ouch!" He rubbed at the spot where the cane had landed. "You play ball? If so, I hear the Pirates need a pitcher."

"Get up and walk." Her voice was stern, No one had spoken to him like that in weeks. "I need you to go back to my hometown in Winslow, Georgia. My sister is in trouble."

He struggled to sit up more, and he was a bit put off because she did not help him. He had to do it for himself. Some caring nurse she was. He did recall that she had been an activist in Georgia, having the nerve to protest lynching and low wages. Practically had been chased out of town for her protests. "What does that have to do with me?"

"A famous journalist like you can shed light on her case and bring some justice down there. You can also bring her back up here for me so she can help with the baby."

"I can barely walk. I'm not some kind of chauffeur. Or nanny."

"Start practicing. Take the train down there."

"I don't want to ride the train."

Ruby fixed him with those eyes again, then her look softened. "I can't do it. Adam said he would tie me to the stove." Her hand went to her belly, a sight full of longing and beauty, and it hurt him to look at her. "I don't want to lose this baby."

A pang tugged at his heart. His mother had written him about two years ago while he had been away about the loss of a child or two that Ruby had endured. "What's in it for me?"

"What about doing the right thing? What about having a purpose in life?" Ruby demanded, with the soft maternal gaze gone from her face.

"If your sister is anything like you, she won't come with me on my say so."

"She'll come because I need her. I've been trying for years to get her to come up here. She'll do it because I want her to." Ruby handed him an envelope. "Here is train fare and a letter to her. Her name is Margaret Bledsoe. We call her Mags." She stepped back from the bed. "You'll do it, because God wants you to be a man of purpose. There's something for you to report down there in Winslow, but if you don't go, you won't get the story."

The confusion entered his voice and made it crack a little. "What story?"

Ruby turned on her heel. "If I told you now, you wouldn't go." Ruby put a hand to her back, rubbing a spot there. "Come on, A.T. Caldwell. I never told you this, but we used to read your pieces at night, looking forward to getting the *Pittsburgh Courier* with such excitement, wondering what you had done next. You made the race proud. You can do it again."

"I can't go down and ask some strange woman to come to Pittsburgh with me. It wouldn't be proper."

"Go to the Winslow cotton mill and get a job there. She's one of the ones in charge. You'll see the injustice." He hated to admit it, but his curiosity was engaged. A Negro woman in charge of the mill? Who was this Mags Bledsoe? Ruby came back to the side of the bed, grasping his hand in her small one. "You aren't the only one difficult things happened to. Think of Job. I used to think of him. I was shunned when my virtue was stolen to silence me. Be a strong man of God in the face of trial."

All he could think of when Job came to mind was someone who was way too long winded. He peered closely at her. Sister Ruby had a story, too, and she had just shed some intriguing light on it. What could he say to this expectant woman grasping at his hand, begging for his help? What was the story? Did she know her request was a deck chair from the Titanic that was his life? Should he grab at it? "Does your sister resemble you?"

"No." Ruby grinned and pulled her hand back, with her lovely face softening with love. "She looks even better than me."

He'd had enough of adventuring, but he had to do this. To help. His missing leg started to ache again, but he swallowed and refrained from touching it. Fine. He would find out the story and see this Mags woman back to Pittsburgh. Then, he would come back to his room and seek the privacy and quiet he longed for.

Just her name, Mags, irked him, but he had never shirked his duty of helping women when called on—it was the price he had to pay for being the only boy in the middle of a sea of sisters.

Winslow, Georgia— three weeks later

"Turn in your time card. That's the end of your time as manager."

Did Mags's mouth hang open as she faced her boss, Paul Winslow? Dignity, always dignity. She pushed up on her chin with her hand. "What do you mean?"

"I mean, girl, get your time card so's you can get paid the last of the management pay. I told you this wasn't permanent. This is it for you."

"May I ask why?" She drew herself up to full height, hoping to feel and show more dignity, but she genuinely wanted to know. It worked. The older white man cowed, as she had hoped. He knew things at the mill had vastly improved since she had been in management.

"You're still a fine worker, but you need to get back on the line. We got vets coming back from the war who need a job to support their families."

"My job supports my family," she said, thinking of her mother, father and three younger sisters who counted on her. Because of her work, the younger ones could get more schooling than she and her older sister, Ruby, had. Since she had gotten the management job last year, she had dreams of sending them to a college for Negroes. Maybe they could get jobs as teachers or nurses, anything to avoid them having to work in this mill for this man who had been the source of torture for their family.

Paul Winslow folded his hands and looked at her. "You all aren't going to the poor house. Your daddy is doing fine with his farm and pays his taxes on time. He finished putting another room on your house. You don't need the extra. A man does."

Despite the way her mother raised her, she raised her voice. "I don't think you are being fair, Mr. Winslow, 'specially given how I have made this mill run."

"Okay," Paul Winslow seemed to be defeated and there was a little leap in her heart for a minute. "You don't have a college degree."

Her heart sank. What Negro did? She only knew one, her brother-in-law, and he was a doctor—he wasn't going to come back to Georgia and work in the mill. "No, sir, but I don't see how it matters."

"It matters, girl, because I say it matters."

She shifted in her mill shoes and tried to look downcast, but a fire burned in her belly. Even more mean and ornery since his wife Mary had died last year, he had to be dealt with gently. "Who is it?" she asked, "No one around here has a college degree."

"I'm bringing in a new man. One of your people, so's you all will mind what he says do." Paul Winslow stepped from behind his desk and opened the door. "Come on in, Mr. Thomas."

A tall man with broad shoulders stepped forward. He wore a suit with a tie and a properly stiffened celluloid collar. She had never seen a man, a Negro man, with skin the color of a fine beef gravy. Deep and rich. His hair lay close and curled on his head, and was black. He had a slim moustache. Walking in with a cane, he had a slight affected limp. He looked like a man of leisure, and not a worker. His hands and the nails on them were impeccably groomed. It made her want to stuff her unkempt hands in her apron, where no one could see them. Was Winslow serious?

"Hello," the man said in an impossibly deep voice that despite her best efforts, pulled a taunt string deep within her. "Nice to meet you."

He held out his smooth non-laboring hand.

She turned to Paul Winslow. "This man is not someone who can handle the workers. I can tell."

"You're lucky I found someone of your kind to do what is required."

The man stepped close to her, his cologne surrounded her. Nice, like spices.

She cleared her throat. "I'm saying they won't listen to a man in a suit, no matter his color."

"I've had enough talk, Mags. You show the man your job and stand down. Or you'll be fired." Paul Winslow sat down at his desk and waved her off.

After watching every move this man made for four years, she knew when she had been dismissed.

She stuffed her ragged nails into her pockets and stomped away in her heavy boots. "Come on." She closed the door to Paul Winslow's office. "Stay out of my way."

"Yes, Miss Mags."

He loomed over her and she was a little startled. She was the one who was always taller than everyone, and now she had to tilt her head back to meet his gaze. "I don't believe I gave you the permission to call me by my first name. Mr. Paul does it because he is Paul Winslow."

"I apologize, Miss Bledsoe." He bowed slightly at the waist and extended his large hand, with his soft palm up. She swept past him, and he smiled a little. "Please lead the way."

The nerve of him. She couldn't help it—something about this man rubbed her the wrong way and she wasn't going to let him know it. She was in charge of everything, this plant as well as her emotions. She would make sure Mr. Thomas understood the way it was.

She took too much care in her walk, so he could keep up with her. He still had to make adjustments in his movement to accommodate the fake leg Ruby's husband had given him a couple of weeks ago. Should he marvel at her kindness or resent her for being kind? Regardless, as she led the way a little ahead of him, beneath her dove gray mill dress and apron, her tall, slender figure was appealingly feminine and rounded. He shook his head. Better focus on what he was down here for. Mags was coming back with him to Pittsburgh because her sister needed her, but that was all. When they got back, he intended she should go with her family and he would go back to his mother's house and...

Ridiculous just thinking it. A man of twenty-eight years, going back to his mother's house. It was even worse for him, because he was not a regular twenty-eight year old.

"If you are going to work in the mill, you got to pay close attention, Mr. Thomas. The mill's a dangerous place, easy to mangle a hand here." The sparkling black eyes of Mags snapped with fury.

"I appreciate the warning, Miss Bledsoe, but I'm used to working in dangerous circumstances."

She seemed to take notice of his leg and had the good grace to be embarrassed. Then she looked back up at him and her direct tone stirred something pleasant in him. "I never told you my last name, Mr. Thomas."

"No, you didn't." He smiled at her. She was quick. He liked her combination, a delicate beauty with a steely disposition and a quick mind. She would be a treasure for some man.

"Who are you?"

"My name is Asa Thomas, like Paul Winslow told you." It wasn't a lie. Those were his first two names. He left off the Caldwell. Many people, especially those of the Negro race knew who he was from his journalistic endeavors. He wanted to remain circumspect until he found out what he needed to. Also, he had a sneaking feeling that this quick wit of a woman would not respect him as a mill manager if she knew he was a journalist. Still, his experience in the military in lining up food supplies and deliveries for soldiers was bound to come in handy here. That was the experience he had told to Paul Winslow and he had hired him on the spot.

"And?" Her black eyes narrowed.

"Your sister Ruby sent me down here. She thought you might need looking after."

Mags clapped her hand on her skirt. "I knew it. I knew it. That girl can't keep her nose in her own business for two seconds. If she were here in front of me, I would strangle her!"

Despite himself, he smiled at her. "There's no need for your reaction. She's your sister and she loves you. She wants you to be well taken care of."

"Typical big sister reaction. I can take care of myself and the family by myself, thank you."

"It must be a heavy burden, to take care of a family."

"I do what I have to. Did Ruby know you came to take my job? Wait, she probably did. She never approved of my promotion, even though it meant more money for us."

"Mrs. Morson is smart. And caring."

Her eyes softened. "How is she?"

"She looked fine last week."

"She better be taking care of herself. I'll go up there personally and strangle her."

"Hmm. The second time you bring up committing a crime. You don't sound as law-abiding as you appear, Miss Bledsoe. Besides, your sister would like nothing better. She directed me to bring you to Pittsburgh when I'm finished with my assignment here."

Her eyes brightened. "You don't plan to be here forever?"

He could have shot himself in the leg all over again. What was it about this woman who made him open himself to her in such an increasingly vulnerable way? He stepped back, leaning a little more heavily on his cane. "No. I'll get the mill to be more productive and profitable over this summer. Just three months."

Her brow furrowed. "I had been doing my job for a whole year before you ever stepped foot in here." Then she was embarrassed again at her reference to his foot. "I apologize. I'm usually better behaved than this, but it's not every day some strange man comes in here to take my job from me and tell me my sister wants me to come to her in the cold north."

"As I said, I won't be here forever."

"My family needs the money, despite what Winslow thinks."

"Don't you want to see your sister and help her with the new baby?"

Her beautiful jewel-like eyes softened again. "Yes, I would. But I have always said to Ruby, I would come on my own terms. I cannot be spared here."

Despite himself, he stepped closer to her. "She believes you are in danger here."

Her fringed eyelashes swept down her cheeks rapidly. "It's like Ruby to make more of things. I'm fine."

"Maybe Paul Winslow is dangerous to work for?" He was on the verge of getting more information.

Mags waved her hand. "He would never touch me. I'm his line to information about his grandson. He wants to know about Solomon as much as possible, but he doesn't want to ask Ruby or Adam. Having me run his mill is cheaper and he has access to it all, along with any little update about his family he needs."

Solomon was Paul Winslow's grandson? The best behaved four-year-old he had ever seen? Asa cleared his throat, holding back on the heart pounds he felt when there was something exciting involved. The story. There was much, much more here than Ruby had let on. Now he understood. Mags's proximity to the mill owner made her a potential target, as her sister had been. Still, he could not resist helping a damsel in distress, especially when she didn't see the danger herself. It was how he had gotten into trouble once before, but he was willing to risk himself to help, even though he had paid a heavy price.

Besides, he could tell Mags Bledsoe was worth it.

Chapter Two

Asa Thomas attended well to her explanations of how the machines worked. Too well. He was coming in to take over, she just knew it. She avoided his gaze as he spoke to her.

"You've made a good show of things here. What's your background?"

Mags colored a little. "I'm not sure what you mean."

"Where were you educated?"

Now she met his gaze. "Winslow is a mill town with a beautiful little school on one side of the train tracks for white children. For the Negro children there is the little schoolhouse that doubles as First Water Church for Negroes. That's where I went to school for eight grades. When Adam Morson came and Ruby started to go to high school by correspondence, I took up her studies too. It took me longer after they moved up north, but I finished last year."

"There's no high school here for Negro children?"

She wanted to laugh at his question. "The Negro children here are lucky to get the eight grades that the law says they are entitled to between the cotton and the mill." She grew serious. "There are many here who think that educating a black woman is a waste of time. My parents never felt that way."

"That's remarkable." Asa kept writing in his little book. "And their efforts paid off. What you have done here is very singular without a formal high school education or college."

"Thank you?" How could she sound so questioning? This man wasn't anyone special.

Asa closed his book. "There are some things that can be done here, but I can start on Monday."

"We are at work now. We work at the mill from six to six during the week. Today, Saturday, we work from six to two. If you want time off already, then that is fine."

His chiseled features, covered in a rich smooth brown, hardened when she mentioned the hours they worked. He corrected her. "I wasn't looking for time off, only a fair according. It's incredible that you work that hard. Hasn't Paul Winslow heard about Teddy Roosevelt?"

She shrugged her shoulders. "Who hasn't?"

"I mean, in other places, like Pittsburgh, they are working eight hours a day during the week only."

"Not on Saturdays?"

"No." She focused on a portrait of George Washington on the wall as he made more notes in his book.

She swallowed hard. Ruby lived in a fantasy world up in the cold North. How could she think of sending someone down here who wanted to change things so drastically? Two whole days to themselves? To do what? Mags shook her head. Most of the Negroes would be drinking or getting into trouble.

But what if she could do whatever she wanted? To go shopping or on a walk with a man? Mags straightened her back, and her corset helped her in the endeavor. There would be no more of that for her, not since Travis died.

She cleared her throat. "What would someone do with all of that time? And less money. We have to make a living."

"Whatever you wanted. Spend time with your family. Spend time with a special someone on a walk. Things a young woman like yourself would like." How had he read her mind? Warmth spread through her as he fixed her with his sharp gaze, black eyes on her. She made an effort to stop warming up as he stared at her. How rude. He had no business coming in here and reading her thoughts in that way.

"There's money to be made."

"You sound like Paul Winslow." He showed his splendid white teeth while nodding his head.

She straightened out her skirt, trying to warm her legs and avoid the cold chill that swept through her as she remembered poor Travis's fate. "I hope that you aren't coming here to make trouble. My sister is someone who could have told you about what happens to those of us around here who get into trouble."

"I've heard. It was just last month, wasn't it, where there was a terrible race riot and lynching in the next county over. Three men burned to death. Yes, I know."

Thank you, God, he's not foolish.

How sad it would have been if this mustachioed man was as naïve as her brother-in-law when he first came to Winslow.

Still, why was she thinking of his black moustache that was so neatly trimmed? He needed to know a thing or two about the way things worked around here. "Good. Then you'll do what needs to be done and not try to reduce our hours down here. Paul Winslow won't like it."

Asa closed the book again. "What if you were paid a living wage to work a forty hour week? How would that be?"

"Idle hands make light work for the devil," Mags quipped. "We have better things to do here in Winslow by making the mill more profitable."

"We'll see." He immediately sat down in a chair and spread a hand. "I think that there is still some inefficiency here that would make it possible for Paul Winslow to still be profitable and treat his workers better."

Mags burned. Her job as manager meant any inefficiency was her fault. "We live fine here. We have a nice store and a bandshell in town where they play music. Since he left, Dr. Morson has been looking for a doctor to help treat us."

"Negro doctors aren't easy to come by."

"No, they aren't." Mags remembered Adam's brief sojourn in their small town before he was forced to move on. "But he tried. It isn't for strangers to come in and judge."

Now there he was, staring at her again. So impolite. So Northern. A Negro from the South would not stare at anyone in such a direct way. Thomas stood before as proof of what she had heard all of her life. "So, given that it's Saturday, what will you do when you get off work?"

"Off work?" Did such a state exist? She realized that she sounded like a mockingbird out in the Georgia piney woods. How embarrassing.

"Yes. At two." His teeth showed again, mocking her. Lord a mercy.

"I have to help my family. They rely very heavily on me. We keep a boarding room. When Negroes come to town, they stay with us. Usually. We heard nothing of you coming."

"Mr. Winslow is giving me a mill house. It's not very big, but it's good enough for me. I have a car to get around in."

"You can drive a car?" By the injured look on his features, she had questioned his ability. Men didn't like that. "I mean, when Adam left, none of us learned. We parked it in the barn."

"Yes, I drive. It makes better sense for a man with my condition."

"I see. Well. I better return to work."

"You're working as you are talking to me. You didn't tell me what you do to help your family."

"Since you are from the city, I'll explain. We live on a farm. There are lots of chores on a farm to keep busy, especially now. The peaches are due to come in soon and it's a high season for my father. He needs help. My younger sisters are trying to move forward in their own education. I help them. Then I go to sleep. There doesn't seem to be enough hours in the day sometimes."

"I can imagine." Asa stroked his chin. "I can help out if you need it."

What would some Northern Negro know about farming? She inclined her head at him to see if he would like the question back at him. "What's your background? You never said."

"Besides the military? I have a degree in engineering from Lincoln University. That's in Pennsylvania, but on the other side of the state from Pittsburgh."

"Adam went to Michigan for his college."

"I'm acquainted with Dr. Morson's education. He and his family are a fine addition to our church family at Freedom."

Mags brightened. "Is that how you know them?"

"Yes. Your nephew is a delight. Everyone loves him."

Her eyes softened. "I can imagine. He was our baby when he was here for the first months of his life. It's too bad they can't come here. None of us have gone up there yet."

"And why not?"

"Too cold. We've too much to do down here. Ruby understands."

Asa shook his head. "I'm not so sure of that. Why else would Ruby insist that you come back with me?"

"I don't know, Mr. Thomas. For one thing, I'm a spinster. I wouldn't travel with a man unescorted. I couldn't give up my job. I have to help the family. That's the way that it is."

Now he regarded her. Again. Almost as if he were searching her face for something. "I think that she's waiting for you to use your fine mind to understand that there is a better way. You deserve better."

Mentioning Ruby again, he was doubtless wondering what everyone else did. How could such a tall, ungainly, dark-skinned woman be a sister to the short, petite, light-skinned Ruby? She had enough of being compared to her sister—she had been dealing with it all of her life. Enough.

"Thank you. Now, I must be going. Please know that you are welcome to come to First Water tomorrow. It's the only Negro church in town."

"Thank you very much." Asa stood and leaned on his cane. "However, I'll be seeing you much sooner than that, Miss Bledsoe."

She had done her Christian duty in inviting him and now, she wasn't sure how to respond. Educated people, besides Adam, made her feel very uncomfortable. Maybe it was because he had a real college degree in what she was trying to do there at the plant, and she was pretending.

She nodded and walked away from him, trying not to be consumed by his last comment.

When the whistle blew later that afternoon, Mags gathered up her lunch pail and shifted her thoughts to the next task ahead—getting dinner ready at home. There were ham steaks that were in the icebox, ready to be fried up for dinner. They would be quick and filling. She could make a peach sauce for the of knowing her?

But why not?

Because, how could he do what he needed to do in supporting a woman, let alone a family with a leg like this? He certainly couldn't travel and get stories as he used to. How could he play with a child or be its father? He didn't understand why no one else could see these problems, as he did, but he couldn't worry about that.

He approached John, who was brushing down a mule. "Mr. John."

"Mr. Thomas. Asa. What's going on?" John seemed surprised to see him there.

"There was an incident at the mill today, and I wanted to ask you some questions."

"Is everything okay?"

Asa related to him what had happened at the mill and discussed Mags's upset. "Well," John stopped to think. "I wouldn't have known it. You must've explained it to her really well, 'cause she wasn't that upset. Her cooking didn't reflect that anyway." John chuckled. "You seem to have that kind of impact on her."

"I thought she hated me because I took her job."

"Maybe some. But she knows that you've come and taught her things that she didn't know before. Mags always appreciates that. She's what you call, a quick study."

"She's that, sir. I wanted to ask, although I think with my reporter's instincts, I know already, that she had a former friend named Travis. What happened to him?"

John stopped his repair and put the bridle down. "Yes. Travis Flint. He always had a bit of a crush on Mags. She never paid him no attention right up until about a month before he died. She started to see him as a man and they began courting."

"Was she going to marry him?"

John gave a little more thought to the matter. "Maybe. Maybe he had asked her. Never said nothing to me about it and by rights, he should have asked me first before he would have asked Mags. But then, he started protesting about his wages at the mill and several men went to his house and beat him up. Took a few days, but he died of his injuries. Sad." John looked up at Asa. "She say something to you about Travis?"

"She mentioned his name when we were driving around last week."

"Well, if you know what I know about how to relate to a woman, you would say nothing about what I said until she tells you. He was just the first one to look at her in that way. Part of what Mags feels is sorrow at his death, and the fact that she waited so long to respond to his courting."

"She spoke about why Paul Winslow needed to be brought down. After what happened at the mill today, I'm inclined to agree."

John looked worried. "That's Ruby talk. We don't need no more of that. This is that man's town. I have tried to have as little as possible to do with him. I live out here on the edge of town so's I can keep an eye on him. I only let my wife do the laundry and carry it back here to do. I don't want her working in that house, and none of my daughters.

"I didn't want none of them going into the mill, but Mags, she insisted that was all the job she could get with her level of education. I keep wishing that I could do more, but it's mighty hard. It was good when Adam came and showed Ruby and Mags how to get their high school diplomas. Nettie's about to get hers and she going to bring the others with her. But once they have them, then what?" He patted the mule. "Maybe it was a mistake since Mags is unhappy and talking crazy talk about bringing down Winslow."

"Why is it crazy talk?"

"He too powerful. She think them mobs is above lynching women, but they not. If Ruby hadn't left out of here... She can't even visit, because she promised the sheriff she was never coming back. I ain't seen my grandson in years because of that." John sniffled a bit. "Now, Mags is going to have to go if she can't just keep her lip buttoned up. Lord, I told her to stay out of that mill."

"Sir, Mags will be alright. In a few weeks' time, when I'm done with my assignment here, I'll take her to see Ruby. I'm sure that we will be able to find a better opportunity for her up there."

John moved around to the other side of the mule and prepared to brush down that side. "That'll be good for her. But bad for us. Don't say nothing, but she's the best cook of any of my daughters."

Asa laughed. "There's still time for the others to learn, sir."

John shook his head. "None of them took to it like Mags. She the best one. You'll be looking out for her?"

"As much as I'm able to, sir." Asa looked straight ahead.

"What does that mean?"

"When Ruby called me down here to investigate, I was still trying to figure out what to do with my life, after my incident." No need to mention that he had had thoughts of ending it. His thoughts just a few weeks ago all seemed so distant and selfish.

"Your leg ain't no problem. You think back in slavery times that the lame slaves got to sit down? No, they still found work in the fields and such. You, you doing the kind of work that you do, writing and such, it won't make no difference to you. They paying you to investigate?"

"Some. And I'm filing stories from them, so that's some more."

"Some and some together. That'll work."

"I still don't know if I could look out for a family."

John gave Asa a hard stare. "Tell me something honest. Was you injured in your manpart?"

"No." Asa could hear all of the nuances of quiet in the barn. "Everything works fine there."

"Then the problem's in your mind. You going to have to decide whether you can get over that or not." John continued to brush down the mule. "It would be a shame to let your life pass based on something that is in your mind. I'll tell you, though, Mags, I mean Margaret. She one of the most patient and kind people I know."

"I can see that about her."

"I don't know if that would make any difference to you, but she's someone you can count on."

"That's the point, sir. I would feel it would be very unfair to put that kind of load onto a wife, when a man is supposed to do all of the heavy lifting."

John gathered up his brushes and put them away. "That girl went down to that mill and showed that white man how he had been doing it wrong for more than twenty years. And you think she can't do any heavy lifting in life?"

"I didn't say that. I just said it would be unfair. Mags could find someone else to be with, some man who was whole and who could do for her as she deserved."

"I see. So she could be some little kept thing somewhere? That's an illusion, Asa. Our women, since back in slavery times, have had to do some heavy lifting. The question is, what'll she do when she gets up to Pittsburgh?"

"That's my point, sir. When she gets there, she'll meet all kinds of men up there who could take care of her."

"So they got more of your kind up there?"

"Some."

"Hmmm. Well, better let Mags decide. Take care, though. I see how she looks at you. Let her down gently then."

"Yes, sir. I will."

John went up to him and clapped him on the shoulder. "And you need to decide if that is worth letting any kind of happiness go because of what is in your mind. Let's go back into the house. Some of the younger ones are going to put on a Bible play. You never know what these girls are going to do next."

"Yes, sir." Asa lingered a bit behind John. After what her father had told him about her, he was surer than ever not to hurt Mags.

If he could possibly help it.

Chapter Eight

Riding home from the mill for the weekend on Friday, the quiet lay between them. Asa disrupted it by asking, "What are you thinking of?"

"I want to make sure that we are ready for the investigation tomorrow."

"And?"

"Well. There's nothing here for me, is there? Winslow is my home, and I won't be able to live here or raise my family here."

Her blunt rhetoric was making him uncomfortable. "You're quite a young woman, Mags. I think you'll be able to do whatever you want."

"Not in Winslow. Because of Paul Winslow."

"I have to tell you, as someone who traveled a great deal before the war, that it's pretty much like this all over the South. Every Southern hamlet has its own boss. Paul Winslow is the one around here. And we haven't made any connection between him and what happened in Calhoun."

"He's done his own dirt here." She fixed her jaw, thinking about poor Travis and how he had died in her arms, injured deep down inside of his body, and Adam not able to help him live. And of Ruby's night terrors and pain.

"We don't have evidence of that."

She turned to him. "We can still confront him."

"I don't think so. We just should focus on what Ruby asked us to."

She folded her arms. She loved the red clay of this Georgia, but she couldn't envision what it would be like to raise a child here. A son, who wouldn't be able to speak up for himself or be beaten down into the grave like Travis. Or a daughter who might have her talents taken from her or worse, like Ruby, her precious virtue stolen from her. She spoke up. "Is Ruby happy?"

Asa seemed jolted by the question. "She doesn't confide in me, you know. She's a friend, but married, and is a part of those married lady circles."

Mags raised an eyebrow. "Really? Married lady circles? She was far more into spending time with the mill men while she was here."

"As far as I can tell, that is not the case there."

"I'll have to see that for myself. I'll go to Pittsburgh and stay there at least temporarily."

"Fine."

"Then I can decide what is best for me from there."

"I think that'll be wise." A careful response from him. He did not seem any more likely to want a repeat of what had happened between them some days ago when he had pressed her fingers to his lips. He had been the model of propriety since. The usual story for her.

If she had been beautiful like Ruby, she might have had a better chance. No, that wasn't true. A warmth ran through her veins thinking of how everyone had talked about Ruby in the wake of her attack—she was too beautiful and David Winslow couldn't help himself. As if her sister deserved to be treated that way and to have Solomon as an unexpected result of the attack. Ruby's spirit had almost completely broken.

No, she should just want to be herself, and not Ruby. Was she still attractive to him?

Or anyone?

Something glowed on the small front lawn of his mill house as he parked his car at the end of the circle.

A small burning cross. No taller than a young child.

All of the mill houses shared a common lawn area that was there for the residents to relax on and to potentially play games like baseball. However tonight, just in the small patch of grass in front of his mill house, was this little love letter. Was it from Paul Winslow or someone else? He ran over to it, but he could see that several men had retrieved buckets of water to pour on the flames.

A group of folk gathered around the front of his house with several of the children crying. Their crying touched a deep chord in him and made him think about what Mags had just said. She was right. She wouldn't be able to raise her children here. He had to help her clear away from such a dangerous place.

"Did anyone see who did this?" he spoke in an upraised voice, although he didn't expect a response.

Instead various people voiced opinions.

"They telling all of us to step on back."

"Maybe we should go to work tomorrow."

"Saturdays off wouldn't last."

He held up his hand. "As long as the mill is still profitable, that's all that matters. It has been even more so. This has nothing to do with the mill."

"What for then, sir?" Katie's tone was not respectful in her use of the title.

He met each gaze in the small crowd before him. One of these people, or more, was a paid spy for Winslow. Had to be. It was why he had built this housing, and why he demanded complete loyalty of the workers. He decided to roll the dice, and said, "There's been a great deal of lynching in this part of Georgia, lately."

They all nodded their heads. Everyone knew this. "Part of why I was sent down here was to investigate it. The NAACP wants to be sure that there is justice in these cases."

"Ain't no justice," Katie's father said aloud from behind her and his wife. "They ain't about playing fair."

He shook his head. "No. But it'll mean that maybe a light shone on these activities will stop it."

"That there cross means, boss, you need to stop whatever you doing. Maybe even leave town."

Asa rolled down his sleeves and retied his tie. "I'm not leaving town. I intend to get to the bottom of this."

"It's starting to get dark out. Best not drive on the roads tonight."

"Thank you for the warning, Mr. Jones. I will be safe. Take your family inside and get your rest. I'll be fine."

"Mags won't like it if you are out too late." Katie gave him half a smile, bouncing on her toes in a strange way.

He returned her smile. "Thank you. I'll be sure to be careful for her sake." Getting back into the car, he understood Mags's adamant insistence about how terrible Paul Winslow was, and now, it was just confirmed for him.

But first, he intended to ask about it.

Asa drove back down the country road to the Winslow house, and tried to think, in a balanced way, of what he would say to him. Still, every time he thought he was being logical, his thoughts strayed towards Mags's words a few hours ago. The yearning in her voice struck him in his heart and he felt her pain at having to leave. Her having to leave made him angrier, rather than logical. How had this happened in just a few weeks' time, his thoughts so comingled with hers that he couldn't react in the normal, rational way? She made him care and now he couldn't back out.

When he got to the Winslow house, he hesitated. Should he go in the back? No. He pulled right in front of the large white mansion. Using his cane to bolster him, he walked up the front steps and knocked as loud as he could on the front door. When the Winslow maid opened the door, she looked scared. "You best go on home from here," she whispered, clearly trying to cover up that he was even there.

Asa didn't care.

"I'm here to see Paul Winslow. I need to report to him that some damage has been done to the mill houses."

Paul Winslow's broad figure emerged behind the scared maid who slipped away as her boss took her place at the front door. "Mighty late at night, Asa. What are you doing here?"

"I'm here to report some damage that has been done to your property, sir, at the mill houses."

"Well. I don't usually respond to that kind of call this late at night. At the front door." The look Paul fixed him with was icy and cold. He didn't care. Asa gave him icy looks right back.

He continued. "A cross burned on the front lawn in front of my house. It frightened the residents and some children were crying."

"Was anyone hurt?" Paul Winslow asked in a measured tone. Interesting. The even distant way he responded confirmed for him that Winslow had known all about it.

"No."

"Good. It seems to me that someone was trying to send a message to someone in the mill houses. Since you are the boss, you best make sure that all of your employees are keeping in line and not taking part in activities that undermine the mill."

"The mill is still profitable, sir."

"People need to stay close to home." A smile broke out on Paul Winslow's face. "Unless, you're courting with a young lady. Nothing like taking a ride in the car with your beloved. But, really, Asa, you shouldn't go too far away. Winslow is Mags's home. It's better to keep her in the confines of this county."

"What's a car for then, sir, if you can't visit folk over in the next county? Or two? Family, relations, what have you?" He didn't like the uneasy feeling that he had when he dealt with Winslow. Reminded him too much of the officer who shot him, and he had to restrain himself from using his cane as a weapon on this man. "That's what the war was fought over, so that people could travel where they wanted."

A dark cloud came over Winslow's face. "That's not what the war was fought over. Just telling you what I think that cross was all about, that's all. Mags Bledsoe is a fine girl and she deserves to have some male company. But she ought to be courting here." He gestured toward the Bledsoe house. "That's why her daddy built that fine big porch. He wanted to have a nice place for his girls to stay with their beaus." He laughed a little. "Of course, his taxes had to be raised up about fifty percent but he pays it. He got a right to a nice courting porch for his girls. It should be made better use of."

"Especially since his oldest daughter never had the chance to use it." Asa stared him down. He wasn't sure if Paul Winslow received his meaning or not, but he was not one to underestimate him.

Paul Winslow kept a blank look on his face and pulled the door closed a little more. "I would invite you in, but I don't like to conduct business at this time. I'll see you on Monday morning at the mill. Good night."

Asa did not return his salutation and went back to his car. He knew that he should go back to the mill house and make sure everything was okay there, but he drove to the Bledsoes', feeling the need for the embrace of the family at this time. Or maybe it was really to see Mags and make sure that she was alright.

A light shone forth from the Bledsoe house when he pulled up in front of it. His heart leaped up in his throat. He didn't want to wake up the whole house, but the noise of the car was sure to wake people up. John opened the front door and Asa gestured to him to come out onto the front porch to talk.

"Paul Winslow left a little something at the mill houses tonight," Asa explained quickly.

"You think it was for you?"

He told him about how Paul Winslow had encouraged him to court closer to home. The set of John's chin looked grim. "I would just as soon ask that you wouldn't go tomorrow. You certainly shouldn't take Mags with you."

"I agree, sir."

As if they conjured her, she was there before him and his fingers instantly slipped against one another. She stood on the front porch dressed in a plaid robe with a white cotton nightgown peeking through. Her feet were bare, and her long thick hair was braided in a single braid. "I want to go with Asa, Daddy."

John shook his head. "You not quite twenty-one yet and you under my roof. I don't like these goings on. Once you're warned, you're warned and that's it. I don't like it at all."

"Daddy, Asa is doing important work. I want to help him with that."

"I want you to be safe."

"Think of all the people that are going to come tomorrow to talk to us."

"They might not even be there if these white folks already know what is going on. Too dangerous."

He stepped apart from father and daughter. "I didn't mean to cause conflict. I just wanted to let you know what had happened and to make sure that you all were safe. I'll go on back."

John put a hand on his arm. "We have the room in the back by the kitchen. You should stay there tonight. You don't want to be out on the open road."

He was about to insist that he would be fine, but the look on Mags's face was transforming. She had been angry as a bull about going into Calhoun, but now, there were tears streaming down her face. "Please, do as Daddy says and stay here." Mags wiped at her face with the back of her hand. He offered up a handkerchief, which she took.

"Okay, Mags. Calm down. It'll be okay." He wanted nothing more than to take her into his arms to stop her body from shaking.

She restrained him, her touch warm and cool at the same time on his forearm. "It was a hot summer night like this when they got Travis. Maybe you shouldn't go back to that mill house. Paul Winslow might use it to control you."

"We can talk this over in the morning, Mags. I didn't mean to upset you."

She had calmed down and took her hand away. "I'm fine. Thank you for the handkerchief." She assumed her take charge manner again. "Daddy, if you can get Asa another shirt to wear, I can wash out this one for him."

John stood up and patted him on the shoulder. "I appreciate you letting us know about this situation."

"You're welcome, sir."

When he departed, he loosened his collar and the night air rushed forward to cool his throat some. Inside, his throat felt parched, but he didn't want to ask her for anything to drink just now. "Sure that you are alright?"

Mags shook her head. "I'm fine."

"We don't have to go tomorrow. I don't want you to fight with your family."

"Do you have your notebook?"

"I do, but—"

"There's a flat board desk in that back room where we study. Once Daddy brings you a shirt, you can go on back there and write about tonight. That's what you need to do. We'll worry about tomorrow, tomorrow."

John handed out a farmer's shirt made of dark red cotton gingham. Not his style at all, but clean. "Thank you," Mags told her father as he waved goodnight and went back inside. "I'll take those." Mags put her hand out to collect his collar and shirt.

The embarrassment rushed to his face all of a sudden but he tried to make light of it, despite the situation. He clutched the front of his shirt and told her, "Turn around."

She did as he said and he quickly took off his usual white boiled shirt and donned the farmer's shirt, which was soft, surprisingly. Buttoning it up, he handed the shirt over to Mags.

They stepped inside together and she showed him where the back room was. She left him standing in the living room where all of the sisters had lined up on the front davenport, all wearing the same nightgown, giggling. Mags came to him with a lamp in her hand, which she handed to him. "For your writing."

He touched her hand as she took the lamp, relishing the brief encounter. "Will you tell me about Travis?"

She shook her head. "Tomorrow."

"I have to know, Mags."

"You need to get to your writing work. Is your notebook in the car?"

"It is. On the front seat"

"I'll send Delie out to get it." Mags pressed her nosy youngest sister into service to fetch the notebook and went into the kitchen. He followed her as she heated water on the stove.

"I would appreciate some of that to wash with," he said. "I feel all grimy from the fire."

"It's no problem."

"Travis."

"Was just someone who came courting once upon a long time ago," she explained without missing a stride in her task. He so loved watching her work.

"He must have been very special to you," he said quietly. Delie came into the kitchen with the notebook and he took it from her with his thanks.

Mags used a paring knife to peel off soap into a pot. "He was a special young man to everyone. I can get this clean, but not stiff with starch in here. I'll do it properly later on."

"That's okay. What made him special?"

Mags stirred the soap and water mix with the end of a stick. "He was just love itself. Everyone loved him and he wanted everyone to have a good life. He was willing to sacrifice himself for that."

"Because he wanted better for you."

She kept moving the soap.

"Because he loved you."

"I told you, he loved everyone."

"But you in particular, Mags," he informed her gently.

"That's what he thought."

"Did you feel the same way?"

"I was too young to understand what he was about. I was about sixteen and he was twenty—the age I am now." She stopped, and seemed to be thoughtful. "It wasn't until he was almost gone that I could even begin to respond. Someone like that deserved better, someone to really love before his life ended so tragically."

"I think that he would have been very happy to take whatever you were willing to give to him."

Mags took the shirts and put them down into the pot. Unshed tears gleamed in her eyes. "I was just somewhere else where he wasn't." She looked up at him. "I vowed not to make that mistake twice in my life."

"You did?" His throat was really dry now.

"When you came here on the porch tonight, I thought something had happened to you. I thought the same thing had happened. What you're doing is too important for them to get to you. You cannot be lynched. We can think about tomorrow, but you, Asa, and me too, we have to get out of here to tell the story without anything happening."

"I would agree." He laughed a little, but he could see that Mags was serious.

She poured a basin of hot water and handed it to him. "You can wash up in that back room and set the pan outside of the door. You need to write."

Her hands slid against his as she handed him the basin. Did she, could she care for him? What was he going to do about it? His hands got slick all of a sudden and he gripped the basin tighter to avoid making a bigger mess than the one he already created.

Chapter Nine

When Asa emerged from the little back room off the kitchen dressed in laid-back dress the next morning, his intentions were clear.

He was going. Not too fancy, just as James told them.

She had taken out an older white shirtwaist to go with her tan work skirt. But, as a special touch, instead of boots, she would wear her high button shoes. She wanted the people in Calhoun to see that she cared about their predicament, and that she was the necessary part of the team. She turned over the bacon. "Morning."

"Good morning, Mags. Got coffee going?"

"Yep."

"I'll need it. I got a lot of writing done last night. Or this morning."

"Wonderful. Help yourself. There's plenty." Mags put the bacon on a plate and sliced some new to fry. "Too bad that I don't know how to drive, I could help."

"Maybe we can fix that." Asa smiled and as Lona bustled in saying good morning to both of them, she expressed her disapproval.

"Women don't belong knowing how to drive. I couldn't get at Ruby to correct her, but I'm surprised at you Mags. Your manners are better."

She gestured at Asa over her mother's shoulder. "Maybe not, Mama. Asa says that Ruby is a part of sewing circles and everything up north."

"I would have to see that for myself." Lona pulled down bowls and quickly pulled together a biscuit dough, shaping large cathead biscuits like magic from the tips of her fingers.

"That's why I'm going up to see her."

"And why you are going to be here with me this morning. I need your help getting some things ready for the canning and for the Fourth of July in a few weeks. Then, we got to get ready for the revival in a few more weeks. Remember, they didn't have it last year because of the influenza."

She remembered. It would be nice again to see Brother and Sister Carver, who, despite their advance age, still made time to come to Winslow because they loved the Bledsoe family. They had special relationships with Ruby, and might have news from her. "I know, Mama. But Asa needs my help today."

Lona looked at her with her eyes blazing. "Why are you trying to be alone with him all of a sudden, when this is the man who took your job from you? Is he asking something of you?"

"No ma'am." She jerked back a little, startled at this angry sudden turn from her mother.

"Then you can do as your family wants and stay here. It might be one thing if he could protect you, but he can't."

"Mama!" She breathed out, in astonishment. She wanted to open a hole in the red earth and crawl in, not for her mother, but for Asa, who had heard what she said.

"Excuse me." Asa slipped out onto the back porch.

"Mama, you hurt his feelings." Tears started in her eyes at the wounded look on his face.

"Things are different. Better his feelings hurt than my child," Lona said blandly.

"Lona, in all of our years together, I have never seen you be so disrespectful to a guest in our house." Her father had appeared in the doorway of the kitchen, frowning.

Mags lifted the burned bacon from the pan. Her parents never confronted one another in such an open way. They got along so well. Their daughters would laugh and say that their parents never, ever argued, but she could see how angry her father was.

Lona put her apron to her face, her usual posture when she was going to cry and sure enough, her mother didn't disappoint. "What could I do? Mags is bound and determined to go off with this man. I never seen her like this, my most obedient child, the one I lean on the most, Mags is my backbone. What would I do in this world without her?"

"Woman, you got three other daughters."

"Why does people say that when someone have five daughters? They're each precious. Didn't we name them all after jewels?"

Mags felt like a fifth wheel on a wagon standing there frozen while her normally unexpressive mother talked in such an open way about how she felt about her. She went and put her arm around her mother's shoulders while she sobbed. "Mama, please calm down. It isn't good for you to take on like this."

"I'ma 'pologize to Mr. Thomas, 'cause I want him to be comfortable here, but I can't apologize for wanting to keep my child out of harm's way. Everything around here getting ramped up so, it would be better if everyone just stayed at home."

"Mama, these people getting brave. They are going around to folks' homes doing their dirt. They burned down the church over there in Calhoun. What about what God would have to say about protecting his house? We can't have them coming around here and burning up First Water."

"No, we couldn't." Lona wiped at her eyes.

"Mama. We're going on a picnic. That's all. A drive and a picnic. Then we'll be home."

Asa's presence hovered off of the back porch and her father stepped forward to invite him back into the house. "Once you all eat, you can be on your way."

He started to open his mouth to exclude her, but she nodded her head at him. "Mama's all right now."

"I am. I'm sorry for the things I said, Mr. Thomas. Please. I don't want you to be uncomfortable at my table."

"That's all right, ma'am."

Mags gestured to him that he should go out and sit at the table and with a half-smile, and he did.

Passing her father the platter of half-burned half-cooked bacon, she patted him on his arm in silent thanks for allowing her to go.

Asa didn't want Mags to think that he was still angry, so he forced himself to make pleasant talk with her.

But he was.

Still, how could he be angry at Mrs. Bledsoe, when her thought so clearly and openly expressed his own fears? What right did he have to speak against her when that was the way he felt himself? He wasn't a whole man, so how could he present himself to Mags as someone who could take care of her and any children that they may have, regardless of what her father had said?

He saw his mistake. He had allowed himself to have hope, especially after his conversation with John, but Lona's strong disapproval of him put that all to rest. He forced himself to keep his eyes on the road. He was doing enough by coming south and making life better here in Winslow for Mags, for her future, for her family—the one here now and the one sure to come. That was his purpose. It wouldn't be fair to her to ask for more.

Driving up a back road and turning the corner, he saw that part of the church had been hauled away. He smiled. People might assume that the Negroes of Calhoun were simple and not bright, but he would beg to differ. This was a natural reason for them to get together. Who would begrudge them the right to rebuild their own church? It was the perfect reason for folks to gather. And talk. He parked next to the parsonage and helped Mags out of the car.

James saw them and waved them over. "Howdy folks. Glad to see you."

"Glad we could make it." Asa shook James's hand. "You got the perfect reason to gather. Perfect day for it."

"Might as well. They don't like it if too many Negroes are in one place. But they can't take away our right to Praise God." James gestured to his cabin across the road where women bustled busily and laid out long tables decorated with gay red gingham cloths that matched his farmer shirt. "Annie be looking for you,

Mags. She over in there."

She touched him lightly on the arm. He couldn't help it, he still felt warm when she did that, despite the late June day. "Will you need me here?"

"I'll be fine. Go ahead. You get a different perspective," he said, and as he did, he wished that he had given her a notebook. Part of what he admired about her was her precision, and no doubt, she would be great at taking her own notes.

Making a mental note of it, he made sure she would get one if they had to continue these investigations. He watched the way that she moved across the roadway with her light skirt swaying, waving a hand at Annie and some of the other women. She would be a wonderful help to any man lucky enough to have her.

"A really nice young woman. She come from a good family, that's for sure," James commented.

"That's true. Having met all of them, I can say that they are quite wonderful. As is she."

"Yes, I can see you thinks that."

He waved a hand. "She's just my assistant on these investigations and we work at the mill together. That's all."

"Maybe that's what you think, but I sees how you looking at her. And she you. She like you."

"She's young. Never been around too many like me, and so she likes me."

"Hmm. Maybe."

"Mags deserves someone who can do wonderful things for her. She might even meet a young man here today who would be willing to pay court to her." Even as he spoke the crazy sentence, a pang echoed in his heart as he walked with James to the former ruins of the church. There were a number of men collected near the church, healthy-looking men hauling away burned items, sawing wood, hammering nails and such. Plenty of strong whole men, all available to escort Mags somewhere. Watching their furious activity made him want to sweat in the early morning sun.

"They's no doubt of that. She a fine figure of a woman. I was talking about you." James fixed him with a look.

"She doesn't want a beat-up old man like me." Asa tried to laugh but it hurt too much.

"That's not how she's looking," James argued.

"Regardless."

"I don't know what that means, but you gots lot to offer a woman. The war is over. We got us a new war here we fighting and you're a plenty strong warrior with your words. I set up a bench up here where the men can talk to you and take a break at the same time."

Sitting and talking wouldn't get the men to open up to him. "I appreciate that, but I have a better idea. I can hammer nails with the best of them if you'll have me?"

James brightened. "We needs all the help we can get. I thank you kindly, sir."

Asa rolled up his shirtsleeves, taking himself away from what he was used to, and put the notebook down on the bench, ready to work.

As he knew, the men were much more willing to talk about their disgruntlement when they were working. He learned a great deal. He was glad though, when Mags came over for a water break. She came to him first.

"How're you doing?" She handed him the tin cup of water. He drank it down, loving the spring water they had here in Calhoun.

"Learning a lot and being useful." He decided to take a break to take some notes. He went over and picked up his cane and notebook off of the bench and followed her to the long tables set up in James's yard.

"Looks like I'll have more washing to do." Mags grinned at him.

"If it comes to the kind of story I want to write, I could hire someone."

Mags shook her head. "No, I can do it. As the best laundress in Winslow, my mother doesn't come as cheaply as I do."

He wished he could take her by the hand as they walked across the roadway in a companionable silence.

Why did I say that? Her humiliation was like dry cake in her mouth.

From a distance, she watched as he took in ham, beans and cornbread. There was no need to try to be friendlier with him. He clearly kept pushing her away as if he were sorry for the day when he had her fingers to his mouth and kissed them. Her mother this morning probably made it worse.

Standing at another table, Mags took a knife to a peach pie, ready to cut it evenly into eight pieces. Annie came and stood beside her, watching the men eat as the women did. They would clean up after the men and they would eat as the men returned to work. "There was some time this morning where my Mama didn't want me to come," she admitted. "But I couldn't stay away. They have to see God's people cannot be kept down. To burn a church, well, that's sin itself."

Annie nodded her thanks at a passing woman whose name Mags had forgotten. "I don't blame your mama. These are bad times. Too many want to do us harm. But you came anyway?"

"Asa needed my help."

Annie smiled in a too familiar way. "I see."

She shook her head. "No, ma'am. It isn't like that."

"It isn't?"

"He doesn't like me like that."

"And how do you know that, missy?"

"He says I'm his assistant, and I help him at the mill."

"Ain't no better way to come together, in my opinion."

"Maybe, but that's not what he says." She put the cutting knife down. "I only knew Travis. He was always saying how he felt about me and how he loved me."

"Travis?" Annie frowned. "That name sound familiar."

"Yes, ma'am. He was murdered about four years ago in Winslow. He was with my sister, asking for better pay. He had the idea that he was going to fix up a home for us and he wanted more money. Paul Winslow's bad men didn't see it that way and they beat him up because of it."

"And then he died?"

She lowered her head and Annie patted her on the hand. She handed Mags a stack of smaller tin plates of various shapes to put the peach pie slices on. After she dished up all the pie and they handed it out to the men, Annie came back over to her and put a hand on her shoulder. "You know, your Asa, he been through a lot with the war and all. He might be quiet about the things he thinking. You need to give him more time."

"He's not mine." She laughed. "And he has important work to do. I shouldn't be getting in the way of it." She sobered. "The whole country needs to know of the wrong that is going on here."

"You're mighty right about that." Annie put a hand on her hip. "We got to find a way to live our lives where they ain't stepping on our necks all of the time. You, you and him, you young. Give it time. He'll come around."

"He's got to finish at the mill for a few more weeks and we can go up to Pittsburgh. I'm going to help my sister with her baby when she comes."

"That's good getting to know each other time."

Mags waved a hand. "When we go back, he'll find someone else up there in the north."

"He ever say he had someone up there?"

"No." She puzzled. "He didn't." She put her head down at the memory, embarrassed. "He did say he was a man, and he had a man's needs and not to play around."

"Hmmm," Annie said with a smile on her lips. "Sound like potential to me."

She pushed her lips together, shaking her head. "I'll start clearing plates." She went to the table and made herself useful, as she knew how to do. She noticed, though that Asa's eyes followed her as she worked and she gave some thought to Annie's pronouncements. Could it be possible that Asa liked her beyond being a worker in the mill or a helper in his investigations? Taking the dishes back to the sink, she got about the work in getting them clean in the dishpan.

"Hmm, hmmm." Annie carried in another load of dishes. "He just ask me if you are okay."

"He hasn't seen me for a while out there."

"He know you are okay. *He* wants to know how *you're* doing," Annie said putting emphasis on the words he and you're. Mags laughed at Annie's shenanigans.

"That's nice, Annie. No matter what you thinking."

"Didn't he just say to you that you better not play with him, that he's a man?"

"He said that last week."

"Yes. See, that's him saying that when you are ready, he going to take it all the way with you. Excuse me, I don't want to speak about the deceased, but Travis sound like a little boy, declaring his love for you all the time and everything. This here is a man who been to the war and seen some things, and he didn't never say anything about another woman."

The stillness in the room made her realize that about four other women besides Annie were listening to Annie talk.

"That's it. He like you," one of the older women butted in and when she did, Mags remembered her name was Lizzie. "Like a man likes a woman."

"He just wanting a welcome from you," Annie insisted.

"A welcome?"

"You got to do something, let him know he's welcome." Lizzie sliced down more ham for the women to eat and all of the women giggled.

"What?"

The laughter grew and filled the room. Except for her.

"She know when the time come." Annie waved them off. "We is hungry, serving up these hungry men. And we got dinner to make too? Let's go eat. While we eat, we can think of something to help our friend here with her man problem."

"That ain't no problem," one of the younger women, Reena, said. "That's easy."

"Easy for you to say." Mags eyed the cooling dishwater that had a layer of congealed ham grease and bean juice floating on top. She went to heat more hot water in the kettle.

God must have sent Asa by way of her sister to escape Winslow. She needed him to figure out how she could impact Paul Winslow enough to destroy him, but not his business. Her brother-in-law and nephew, as his only living descendants, still drew dividends from the mill.

When the time came, there might be another man who would stay by her. By that time, when she accomplished what she needed to do, the newspaper man would be long gone after some other story.

A funny feeling rolled around her stomach at the thought of her life without him, but that was reality.

She had better get used to it.

Chapter Ten

"A wonderful day." Asa broke another silence between them as they rode back from Calhoun. "Thank you for spending it with me."

"You're welcome." Mags played with her handkerchief, always keeping her fingers occupied. He started to whistle, but then stopped.

"I think I'll get back and write this out, so it stays fresh in my mind."

"Sounds like a good idea. That's why Annie gave you a nice plate of leftovers. You can eat and get a lot of work done back at the mill house."

"You think I am going back there?"

"That's what it seems like."

"No, I think that you Bledsoes are stuck with me until I leave. I mean, when *we* leave for up north."

"That's nice." Mags stared off to the side of the road. What was going on? She wasn't happier that he would be around a bit more?

"Yes. Winslow can keep his mill house and the money he's taking from me to live there if I cannot be safe and unthreatened in my own home."

"Makes sense."

"Glad that you agree."

She whipped around to face him. "Do you think there will be any more lynchings around here?"

"Hard to say. We're engaged in a risky investigation right here."

"I know. I don't like that there is so much danger for people, and so much hurt for the families."

"Did Travis leave family behind?"

She gave a thoughtful pause. "No, nobody. His mama had died the year before— God is merciful in some ways because his killing would have about killed her. I think it was one of the reasons why he was so willing to take on that risk, because she was gone. He might have been more careful if she were alive." She brought the handkerchief up to her face, shedding a few tears.

Clearly, she was still enamored by this Travis fellow, and he was glad. He sat himself straighter as he drove. Really. Her great love for the deceased Travis freed him from feeling more responsible for her and it made it all the easier for him to say goodbye to her when it was all said and done. The hollow feeling inside of him probably could be filled with more dried apple pie.

"Did you ever have anybody to love?"

Now it was his turn to whip his head around. "What made you ask that question?"

"You told me," Mags said evenly as if he were a child, "you were a man and that you were not to be toyed with, and had a man's needs. You been away to war and injured and everything. You aren't too bad to look at. It stands to reason that you would have somebody, 'less all the girls in Pittsburgh are fools."

Asa wanted to laugh out loud at her nerve and tenacity. She was something. All of her reasoning made sense and was quite in line with reality. Once again, another reason to admire her fine mind. He took in a deep breath, ready to confess. "I had a fiancée."

"I thought so," Mags said half smiling. "You used the past tense. Did you break up?"

"Aline died in the flu epidemic."

"I'm sorry."

"She died in my arms."

"As Travis died in mine."

They were both quiet as the realization dawned on him that they had this in common as well. Anything more that he had in common with her frightened him. He did not want to be closer to her.

"Well, it would appear that we had some sad times in our lives." There.

That would wrap up the moment.

"I've asked God many times to help me about Travis. So much of what I think about and do is about getting Paul Winslow back for the role that he played in killing Travis." He looked over and saw that there were tears running down her cheeks. *Stop. Stop.*

He gripped the steering wheel. He did not want to be impacted by her. He did not want to have feelings for her.

Too late. He pulled the car over onto the side of the road.

"Every time I try to do something else, or think about something else, I'm so mad. It's a prison. I want to be free of it."

He reached out and she went into his arms with her tears wetting the front of his farmer shirt and making it quite wet and soggy. Stroking her cloud of hair, he didn't care. She should not be upset anymore. There had not been any other woman in his arms since Aline took her last breath more than a year ago. Somehow, he carried a curse in his person and he wanted Mags to be free of him.

So he pulled her away to face him. "Look, you loved Travis and he loved you. Keep thinking about young Negro men being free of the chains of men of power like Paul Winslow. It's time for that treatment to end. We're all coming back from the war and we want to be treated like men. Like how it was in Europe."

Mags sniffled, and edged over again, restoring herself. "How were you treated in Europe?"

He'd better do something else before he lost control, holding her like that. Taking the opportunity to pull his arm back, he maneuvered the controls to start the car. He made his arm muscles rigid and strong because he didn't feel strong inside, holding her soft, sweet smelling body so close to himself. Shifting in the front seat, he steered the car out onto the road again.

"Are you okay?"

She nodded her head. "How was it?"

"We were treated like, like human beings. All of the things you think about, even now, about how we couldn't stay for the dinner because it would have been too dark to go home, that doesn't exist over there. Women don't look at you in horror as you walk down the street past them. They're friendly and say hello."

"Is that how you met your fiancée? Aline?"

Asa nodded and his mind wandered a bit. "We met in a café. She worked there, and I liked to go there to eat and write. See what I mean? Here, in the wonderful United States, we have to think about where we can go to eat. There, you do not."

"My goodness." Mags put a hand to her chest.

"One time, she asked me what I was always writing and I told her. She seemed very sympathetic to the plight of the Negro soldier. The café was owned by her parents and people like to go there to have celebrations. When the troops were about to leave, she had a moment where she told me that she liked me very much and wanted for me to stay. I promised her I would be back after covering the events on the front. That was when I was shot by the commanding officer and I had to have a place to heal after the hospital. Her parents took me in. There was no judgment in their eyes when they had to help me with the wound, and they did not hesitate to call the doctor. She fell in love with me. I asked her to marry me and she said yes."

"She said yes?" Mags breathed out. "A French woman?"

"Yes." Asa inclined his head to see if she understood. Given her usual precise way, he could see that she was still reaching and did not grasp it fully.

"She was not a Negro?"

"No."

Now she understood.

She shifted in her seat, grappling with the magnitude of his revelation about his dead fiancée. "I see."

Silence.

"Her family helped me to find the right kind of leg and to walk all over again. They were wonderful to me, as if I were their own son. Their treatment of me was so kind, I was prepared to never come back to the United States ever again. However, the flu came and struck her down. She died within a day."

"I'm sorry," Mags breathed.

"Thank you," he said, with some relief, knowing that she had a heart. "So my praying to God has been of a different sort. I'm in a prison of a kind, too, and I can pray to be free of it, but I know that I never will. You, with your self-imposed prison, you can go north, get more education and be free. You don't have to be at the behest of Paul Winslow all of your life. Think of it that way."

The Bledsoe farm emerged into view and he was glad. This conversation with Mags was very tiring and he wanted to be sure to write tonight. He needed a good meal and energy to help him do that. He thought that he had made her see reason, and to let her know that she had choices in her life, choices that a lot of young Negro women did not.

"What makes you think that you are in a prison?"

She was serious and composed with her hands folded quietly in her lap, not industrious in spite of the white salty traces of tears down her face. The sight jarred him. "I just, I made the comparison because of you know, my injury. It's permanent."

"It is. But did it change who you are? Your mind? What you can do?"

"Well, no, but—"

"Then what gives you the right to act as if it is a prison? When so many of the troops came back poisoned with mustard gas or shell shock? You're a writer and someone with an education. The commanding officer took your leg but he can never, ever take your education from you. He hated you for that. I hope that you won't waste your life because of some hateful man. You owe it to your people to be a beacon of hope for them. You don't have the right to lock yourself away."

Who was this self-righteous, beautiful woman telling him about what should motivate him? Who was she to tell him what he should feel about his leg? She wasn't a man. He breathed again. "That's very harsh, Mags."

"You aren't a farmer or a manual laborer. You have a work, and a purpose. You don't have the right to feel as if you are less. You have a work to do that is meaningful. That's a lot more than a lot of Negroes have."

Asa parked the car and sat there, floored by her words. "Well, I'll just take my plate around the back and begin to work."

"Yes, I think that you better do that." Mags opened the door and let herself out. "I'll let the family know and no one will be offended."

He watched her take her own tin plate upstairs into the front door and heard the warm welcoming sounds of the Bledsoes embrace her and love her. What a wonderful thing to have a family like that, rather than his mother and sisters who were always judging, always thinking themselves above everyone. She was lucky that she had something, people to fight for. She wasn't in a prison at all.

And she made him begin to see that he wasn't in a prison either.

With a few sentences, she turned his entire world upside down, and lobbed a grenade to his sensibility about going back into his mother's room and ending his life.

The entire week, Asa kept his distance from her. Suited her fine. *His name is Mr. Thomas. Caldwell. Mr. Something.*

What had she said that was so wrong? She told him a truth that he needed to hear. She could ask him about his frosty attitude, but she didn't know how to form the words. Even Katie made a notice of it at the mill one day. "He's different. He doesn't act like he did before."

"I know. I think it's my fault." She gave Katie the quick rundown of their conversation.

"You said something he didn't like."

"Well, if he's that changeable, then he might as well finish up here and go back up north and give me my job back."

"You still going up there?" Katie asked, and Mags saw that she was very interested in her response. Well, maybe her young friend would miss her while she was away.

"I don't know. Sometimes, I want to go, but if it means going with old sourpuss, maybe not." They both giggled and then sobered when Asa came walking by, limping a little more because he didn't have his cane for some reason.

Or was he hurt? She smoothed down the hurt in her heart, and instead busied herself putting her lunch dishes back into her pail. She was not ashamed of how she felt. Probably high time someone had let him know about himself. She was not deluded into thinking Asa would be interested in her as some type of wife prospect. She looked nothing like what he had been interested in as wife material.

Besides, that was her mother's own imaginings because the handsome Prince Adam had come into their lives four years ago and swept away Princess Ruby.

No. She was sensible Mags. No one ever swept her away, and she was just fine keeping her feet firmly on the ground. It was too bad that Mr. Thomas could not be grounded in the same sense of reality.

That Friday was the Fourth of July. The mill was closed for a holiday, and since it was, they would have to work on that Saturday to make it up. She didn't mind, as long as they got the work day off. The Bledsoes had the tradition of going into the town of Winslow to partake in Paul Winslow's largess. Mags really didn't want to eat of the too-sweet ice cream that he provided to all who came to see the beautiful fireworks. Still, if she stayed at home she would be there alone with Asa, who wanted to work, and that was not appropriate. She leaned into the small back room. "I left your plate in the warming oven so that you can eat your dinner as you wish."

She put on a pair of white gloves and smoothed down the front of her dress, which was a mauve color. Her large white hat had enough veiling on it to protect her from the sun, but the amount was ridiculous. She had wanted to tell Em to take some of that veiling off, but her sister insisted that was the fashion now, so she had to go around with this big nest on her head. She much preferred the smaller boaters.

Asa had been in his room much of the day, not engaging with the family because he had been working and they were all under orders not to disturb him. He blinked at her as he stood and stretched. She felt more than a little embarrassed at seeing his broad, strong chest peek through his undershirt, and felt a little warm remembering how it felt to be nestled into him when she needed some comforting.

With Travis gone, that would be all she ever had of a man. Once she returned from Pittsburgh and helping her sister, her life as the maiden aunt of her sister's children was set. She would remain there on the Bledsoe farm to take care of her parents to the end of her days. Just thinking of her life provided a kind of reassurance to her.

"Where are you going dressed like that?"

"We had said at breakfast that we were going in for the Fourth of July celebrations. Delie asked you to come and you said that you had to work on your writing." She remembered the singular look of disappointment on her young sister's face and kept a subdued look on her face at Asa's serious countenance when he said nothing in response to her younger sister.

"I've been working on it. I have gotten pretty far today, so I can come and escort you into town."

His curious choice of words struck her and she was about to ask him about it when her mother called her to the front door, dressed in her own finery. "Your father has the mules ready."

"I was just saying goodbye to Mr. Thomas and letting him know about his plate."

"Fine then. Come on."

"No, wait." Mr. Thomas grabbed her arm before she went to the front door and a jolt shot up her arm, making her feel alive as if summer lightening had come down and struck her. "I can drive you in the car."

"I'll go and sit on the porch and wait while you dress." She reluctantly pulled her arm free and went out front. She told her mother what their border had said. Lona looked skeptical, but John waved her concerns off.

"We'll see them there. Look at that hat she's is wearing, you won't be able to miss her." John chuckled, while she fixed her father with a fake angry look at his jesting her.

"We'll see you there soon," Mags said. "I'll sit out here on the porch until he is ready."

With her mother's concerns alleviated because of propriety, the mules pulled off with the three Bledsoe girls sitting in the wagon, waving at their big sister, and probably privately wishing they, too, were waiting for a man on their front porch—even little Delie.

Within about twenty minutes, Mr. Thomas came out front dressed in his finest brown suit and stood next to where she was sitting on the porch. She bit the inside of her lips to keep herself from swooning at his handsome appearance.

"That didn't take long."

"I didn't want you sitting out here all by yourself in your new finery."

She expressed surprise as she stood. "I didn't think that you would have noticed me this week. You've seemed mad at me or something."

"Should someone be mad at the rain?"

"What?"

"You know how after a rainstorm comes and everything is washed away and is clean again? That's what your words did to me the other day. Everything, my injury, Aline's death, made it seem as if my life were a prison. The things you said somehow cleared that away. You're magic, Margaret Bledsoe."

Ignoring the use of her full name, she led the way down the steps to the car. "I'm glad to help."

Asa came around and opened the door of the car and handed her in. "Glad that you were there to help."

After he started the car and came around to the other side, she said, "I think that God places people into your life for a reason."

"And I'm thankful to Him because of it. And to you. Thank you." Asa turned and fixed her with his penetrating gaze.

"You're welcome." Mags kept her voice low because his gaze made her want to take her gloves off so that air could get to her hands. She reached up with a gloved fingertip to wipe an imagined blot from her lips and his hand captured hers, just as it had a couple of weeks ago. "Shouldn't we be going now?" she whispered, his face so close to hers she could see that he had combed his thick mustache and chin hair and that not one hair was out of place.

Not a hair would be out of place, unless... Avoiding her hat, almost as if he had planned it, he leaned into her and a shiver ran down her spine as his gorgeously shaped lips gently but insistently, touched hers.

What should she do? Travis had always acted as if she were a fragile jewel, so precious to really kiss, and so his kisses were light and airy.

Now she did know what that moustache felt like. And no, the moustache did not tickle. She did not feel the least little bit like laughing, even though the thrill pushed down her body to her high button shoetops. Responding with a sigh, she opened her lips up just a bit more.

Then, all of a sudden, cold air rushed in around her mouth.

He had pulled away. "We had better get on to the celebrations." He shifted to pull the car away from the side of the house.

Why had he pulled away? Was it because she hadn't done it right? It wasn't fair. She was only twenty and never had any real practice so that she could know what felt good to him.

Should she ask him for a second chance? Maybe if he stopped the car, he would do it again. She opened her recently abandoned lips, and stopped herself.

Kissing her had made him think of the French woman. She had known how to do it right, and Mags didn't. He probably just wanted to forget that it had ever happened. No need to bring up a painful memory.

With a pain in her heart, she sat back into the car seat and stared down the road again, her mind in a fog.

Because now she knew she falling in love with him.

Chapter Eleven

Asa drove along the road in stunned silence. Had he just kissed Mags? An employee? John Bledsoe's daughter?

And what of her nonchalant, although accepting response? She kissed him as if she enjoyed it, and let him know that she was knowledgeable, but not too much so, about kissing. Oh, yes, she was far from an ordinary country girl. She was every inch a pearl and he wanted her to be on fire for him, to care for him, as he was beginning to care for her. He found himself, Asa Thomas Caldwell, the journalist, tongue-tied as he drove along the road into town.

"You'll want to park the car here," she informed him coolly as they came closer to the town square. "Still, I know that you don't want to park too far away."

"I'll be alright," he assured her in a brusque way, as anger swirled in with his already whirling emotions. Now she was concerned about him, because of his leg? He didn't want her pity, he wanted her regard, her respect and her admiration, and could it even be possible—he wanted her love. He parked the car and sat there a minute, transfixed by the possibility.

What would it mean to be loved by such a pearl? It would mean marriage for sure, and Asa did not know if he could be married to anyone.

Just as he situated to get himself out of the car, she was already out. He couldn't even be fast enough to help her out of the car because she could do it quicker on her own. "Why didn't you wait in the car?"

"I didn't want to." Her response came sensible, calm and rational. It made him even angrier. How could she be so maddening?

"Next time, you are supposed to wait until I come around."

"Why should I?" He saw how perfectly the hat framed her large eyes and clear brown skin, the color of maple -sugar candy.

"So that I could hand you out," Asa informed her.

"We're just going to the Independence Day celebrations. There's no need for ceremony."

"It's not a ceremony to hand a woman out of the car. It's courtesy. It's respect and decorum and thoughtfulness."

Now he could see, with increasing acuity, her rational mind at work. She tilted her head and the hat went to one side. "Is this all about the kiss? Because if it is, I understand. You didn't mean to do it and you want to take it back. Fine. We can go on and act as if nothing ever happened. You've been forgiven. It never happened. Now, let us enjoy the day." She took up a parasol, opened it and began to walk on ahead of him, not slowing for him, leaving Asa dazed and confused.

That was not what he meant! He stood there in a whirl of confusion, leaning more heavily than usual on his cane. He wanted to call her back but everything was happening too fast. He didn't want to take back the kiss and he didn't want her to be angry at him, but he had behaved so badly, he wasn't sure what, if anything, he should apologize for.

"Bring your notebook along." Mags turned around so elegant and fine in her dress and hat. "There'll be many a family coming in from the outer reaches of the county and they may have some things to tell you that could go into the report."

Now she was telling him how to do his job. But, he had to admit, she made too much sense to overlook or ignore her main point, so he brought the notebook, tucking it into his suit jacket and focused on navigating walking along the main road.

He followed Mags to the area behind the main band shell where the Negroes were allowed to gather for the festivities. White families were gathered more around the front of the main band shell and silently, he fumed. People were just barbaric in the way they treated one another. Paul Winslow's entire means was dependent on his Negro workers and how first Mags, and then he, taught them how to be more productive to enrich him. And Winslow couldn't treat the workers any better than seats behind the main band shell, where they wouldn't even be able to see.

The Bledsoe family had set up a picnic table and the sisters spread table cloths and laid out delectable food. Asa knew some of the other families, and he saw Katie come over and make a big fuss over the way Mags was dressed. *High time someone did.* Even though he couldn't do it himself, he was glad that Katie flattered her. She did look breathtakingly lovely. He situated himself at one end of the table and pulled out his notebook.

"This here is the holiday, Mr. Thomas." Katie looked at him and laughed. "What you bring that old notebook for?"

"You never know when you might need to make note of something." He hated himself for being unable to look at Mags in her resplendent dress. She had taken off her hat and her long thick hair was pulled back from her face into a looser bun at the back of her head instead of her usual tight work bun. The relaxed look made her look older than her twenty years, even as Asa reminded himself repeatedly that she was only twenty, and he was ten years older than her.

Out of the corner of his eye, he could see a young Negro man approaching the Bledsoe table and he began to fume. He better not be approaching her, wanting to ask her for a dance, or to come sit as his table or… He saw that the young man palmed a big farmer's hat as he spoke first to John and then to Mags. He bristled as he saw her make a bit of a turn and then brought the young man over to the table and he sat on the bench opposite. "Hello, sir. I'm Alonzo Parker. Up from Harolson County."

He reached across and shook his hand, thinking him a handsome prospect for Mags, but resenting him as a prospect all of the same. "Good to meet you, Mr. Parker." Asa got down to questioning him as a potential husband for Mags. "You have a farm up there in Harolson Country?"

"Yes, sir. I sharecrop up there. I been having a problem with the way the accounts has been kept. Wonder if you can help."

He straightened his leg out. This man wasn't a prospect for Mags's hand in marriage, he was a potential interviewee. He looked up at Mags and saw her bustling around, organizing, as she always did, ready to feed everyone for lunch. She looked over at him and gave him a warm smile. Her smile, when she chose to bestow it, was a wondrous thing, and he felt glad that it was on him at this time, and not Mr. Parker. He turned his attention to some papers that Mr. Parker was drawing out of his hat and fixed the man with a careful look. "There isn't much that I can do about this but to report it as one of those problems that Negros around here have been having."

Mr. Parker smiled as he tucked his papers away as he made some more notes. "God Almighty, I knows. But it feel good to come to an educated man like yourself and figure out what you been feeling is true, and then knowing it is true. I can't do anything about it now, but I been hearing about them jobs up north in the plants. I might could get me one of them and then Mr. Reece don't have me to farm his land. I thank you kindly, sir." They shook hands once again and Mr. Parker went on his way.

Mags sat down in the same place where Alonzo Parker had been and folded her arms over one another. "Lunch is ready. I think you need something to eat, so that you aren't crabby anymore."

"I'm not crabby," Asa informed her as he closed his notebook.

"I can fix you a plate if you like. You keep on writing down what Mr. Parker told you."

"That'll be fine. Whatever you put on it, I know it'll be delicious." He said this to her knowing that she had made the bulk of what was on the table. She went away from him to fix his plate and it was hard to focus on this opportunity to get some things down.

Out of the corner of his eye, however, he saw a white presence hovering on the edge of the shelter, and then recognized many of the Negro families, the ones who had gathered in celebration for the holiday, had grown quiet, watching.

Asa laid down his lead pencil and looked up, seeing an official-looking man, accompanied by another, walking straight for him. He looked up in curiosity. "Good afternoon and happy Fourth of July, gentlemen. Is there something I can help you with?"

"We was just wondering what you was back here doing." He could see that the younger one, who just spoke to him in rather disrespectful way, was probably seeking to make a name for himself. He let out a breath.

"I was just making some notes about the gathering. Probably write it up for the church papers."

"All of these folks been coming to Mr. Paul's Independence Day celebrations for years and know what it is." The older one looked at him levelly and Asa didn't flinch under his gaze. "Just some music, peach ice cream and fireworks. No need to put it in the papers."

"Well, all the more reason for someone like me, who isn't from here, to write stuff down. Where I'm from, we don't have occasions such as this. Wonderful to see." He smiled at him.

"Great. Well, I would suggest that you put away your notebook and enjoy the day, sir." They stared at one another as if it were a contest. He would rather stare at Mags. So, he, with great show, slowly folded away the notebook and put it into his suit jacket.

He eased himself up and made more show of standing up and taking off his suit jacket. In that moment Mags came along and brought him a plate loaded with chicken, salads, sliced tomatoes, a triangle of peach pie and a slice of pound cake.

"You're sure right about that," Asa agreed. "Just the kind of day to enjoy this fine food and some time with your honey." He draped a casual arm around Mags and gave her a big kiss on the cheek. "No big deal."

"No big deal." The older man smiled at him. "Mags is a fine woman—not a trouble maker like her older sister. A fine choice. We'll be seeing you." The two white men walked off and he let out a long breath. Along with everyone else. The startled look on Mags's face at his kiss made him remove his arm from her, even though it felt right and good there.

Now, she let out a long breath. "They never come back here. Ever."

"Really?"

"This is our part. They must have known you were doing something. I didn't mean to get you into trouble. Now they know that you write down things."

"For the church paper," Asa reassured her.

Mags shook her head as John Bledsoe approached them. "They don't believe what you said for one minute. No. They'll be watching. They are always looking at us, ever since Ruby got arrested."

"She what?"

"They arrested Ruby at the Independence Day celebration four years ago. She started reciting the Declaration of Independence along with the Reverend and they took her to prison. She didn't stay in long 'cause Adam got her out."

"Yes, I gathered that she had gotten out at some point," Asa joked, but Mags was not smiling.

"I don't like it, I don't like it if they are looking at you."

He put his hands on her shoulders. "Mags. It'll be fine. Don't worry. Look, if it will make you feel better, I'll keep my notebook out of sight and try to gather information by my mind. I'll even do what I said and enjoy the day. Right?" He then realized that he was touching her right in her father's presence and he took his hands off of her shoulders. "I apologize."

John waved a piece of chicken in understanding.

Mags still looked uncertain. "That older sheriff is the same one who made sure Adam went on the chain gang when Paul Winslow was out of town. It took a while to get him off too. Ask him about it—it was not a good time."

"When I return to Pittsburgh, I will. It seems as if the Morsons were a bit more adventurous than we had ever thought they were." He sat down and began to tuck into his plate. "Aren't you going to eat?"

"I'm not hungry. I'm frightened."

He patted the bench next to him and she sat down, backwards, facing out while he ate facing inward. "I wouldn't jeopardize you."

"What?"

"Put you in any danger."

"It's hard to know now what makes them mad. So many things are going on now, this summer."

John Bledsoe took the seat opposite them and nodded. "Heard there were two more attacks in Nolan and Branch Counties. There's a lot going on here in Georgia that these white folks don't seem to like. Least little thing sets them off."

"Maybe they haven't had any of this good chicken that Mags can make."

John shook his head. "When are you supposed to be done with your assignment?"

"Three more weeks, sir. Then I'll be leaving for Pittsburgh on July 26th." That wasn't that far away, Asa reasoned as he chewed on a flavorful tomato. Would she come with him? "Are you going to come?"

"I'm still thinking about it."

"You need to go on and help your sister." John Bledsoe gestured with his hands. "I know that you won't be chaperoned, but I trust this man. He'll get you to your sister. Think of a way to stay on up there. I don't know what Ruby and Adam can do for you at this point beyond giving you a place to stay, but they might know something. Go on to nursing school like Ruby did. You got your high school diploma, like her. You can do the same."

"I don't want to nurse anyone."

Asa spoke up. "You can do lots of things. I don't think that women can work in the mills up there, but your experience in the mill means you should be able to get something. Maybe domestic work."

A cloud came over John's face as he made the suggestion and as soon as he did, he was sorry. He wanted to open his mouth to apologize, but it was full of peach pie, with its sweetness, crisp crust and sweet spices.

John folded his arms. "My girls don't do day work in no white man's house. That's why I been working like I have. It's okay to do laundry—maybe there is something like that up there where she can bring it back to Ruby and Adam's house, but more than that is too risky."

He understood. "If there was enough time, I would write my mother, and she might know of some opportunity in the church, but I couldn't guarantee a response before it was time to leave."

"She can go on up there to help Ruby and figure it all out when she get up there."

Mags stood. "Glad that you all have this figured out. I have some things to accomplish here first."

"Well, according to your father," he said wiping pie crust crumbs from his lips and moustache with a napkin, "you have three weeks to get it all together. And then we're going."

"What if I have things to do here? What about that? In case it escaped your notice, I am almost twenty-one years old. I don't need you to tell me what to do, I get enough of that at the mill. Once you are gone, I can have my job back and I can go back to earning five dollars a week and go back to helping my family."

He stopped eating. They had suffered a loss in money because he was there? "I apologize. I didn't mean to take your family's money."

Mags waved an impatient hand. "You paid it back with your lodgings, so it all worked out."

"I just think that your father is concerned about you staying down here where things are so heated just now."

"Like I said, I appreciate all of your concern, but I'm almost twenty-one."

"You still under my roof, Margaret Ruth. You'll do as I tell you to. Honor thy father and thy mother that the days of the land be long upon thee."

Mags gave her father a stormy look. Ultimately, John Bledsoe admitted defeat and walked away. Asa had the sense that he did not confront his daughters like that often—it was probably Lona who did that more often, but he knew why John did it. He loved Mags and wanted her to be safe.

"I don't think that your father meant to shout, especially not on a holiday like this. He meant to just let you know that he is concerned for you."

Mags turned on him. "Why did you have to come? Everything here was perfect before you came and now our lives have been turned upside down. Our house was fine, Winslow was fine, everything was just fine before you."

He coughed, saying, "You mean Winslow, the place where Travis was lynched because he asked about the amount of money in his paycheck? Where your sister was attacked and forced to bear a child? That kind of fine, Mags?"

"I'm going to get some of that ice cream," Mags announced and she stormed away from him, toward the front of the crowd and the band shell, going way too fast for him to follow.

Gripping his cane, he knew the kiss he had stolen from Mags's sweet lips just a few short hours ago would never happen again if she had her way about it. Maybe not even the one he had stolen on her smooth cheek.

Suddenly the three weeks that seemed such a short time just a little bit ago, loomed large and long before him.

Chapter Twelve

She would not cry.

He would not receive any satisfaction from her to show that she cared.

She said she was going to have some ice cream, and by gosh, she was going to have some. A memory of how her older sister would chide the annual Winslow ice cream formed in her mind and she had to laugh. Ruby called it "soup time." The whites were all served it first, while it was cold and more than frozen. Only then could the Negroes have a portion, which, by the time they got to it, had been exposed to the hot Georgia weather and was a slushy soupy consistency. Still, it would be a sweet treat, and since the cream their cows produced went to make butter or to sell, the ice cream was a rare treat as well.

She ignored all of the mean looks she encountered from both races as she skirted the line between the area where the Negroes were allowed to the front of the band shell where the whites all sat listening to the music.

There was band music now because of Ruby. It was Ruby's fault they no longer had readings of the Declaration of Independence—now you had to do that at home for your family and yourself before you came to the celebrations.

As she expected, the booth where they dished out the ice cream still had white people waiting in front so she reluctantly took her place at the end of the line, fully prepared to wait her turn to be at least the first Negro to receive the special treat. Still, there were at least fifty people in line and while some people were kind and spoke to her, she could see there were others who were ready to lord their special privilege of getting ice cream ahead of her. She didn't care. It had been two years since she had any, and she was prepared to wait.

The line went all the way to the back of the band shell where there was a small draped area off to the side where performers could get themselves ready to go out on the stage. As she resigned her mind for the long wait ahead, she heard a giggle come from the area.

Katie's giggle. She could not be mistaken because Katie was her friend, and she knew her laugh when she heard it.

Then, she heard Paul Winslow.

Both sounds came from the draped area of the band shell.

She shook her head, thinking somehow that would clear her hearing. Her heart stopped. Paul Winslow said something to her friend in a tone that she had never heard before from him. A sensuous tone. The way Travis used to talk to her to persuade her to be "just a little sweet" to him. While the brief remembrance of Travis made her smile slightly, the fact that she had heard that tone from Winslow and Katie's giggling made her wonder—what were they doing behind that curtain?

Dear Lord.

The contents of her lunch fought their way up her throat. All of a sudden, she didn't feel like ice cream anymore. Pushing her sleeves from her wrists, she made her way back to the safer area where the Negroes were all congregated. She moved back to the tables, wanting to see for herself that Katie was there at her family's table, right next to theirs. She was so busy walking back towards the table that she didn't realize that she had bumped, hard, face first into a broad chest. A pair of hands grabbed her to steady her and she realized that it was Mr. Thomas that she had bumped into.

"Oh," she exclaimed, and pulled her sleeves down, feeling exposed all of sudden.

"Are you alright? Your father sent me after you—he saw no ice cream yet, and he didn't want you getting into trouble."

"I—I." Was she more shaken over the feeling of his hard chest against her face, or over what she had heard behind the curtain? She did her best to gather herself. "Was Katie back there?"

"No, I haven't see her in a while. Do you want me to get some ice cream with you?"

Trying to form an answer, she watched as they saw the two law enforcement officials patrolling the area between the whites and the Negroes again and Asa took her arm in his. They both smiled at the law men who grinned in a terrible way to see their affections. Mags could just assume the lewd presumptions they were making.

"I don't want ice cream any more. Let's go back to the tables to see if Katie is there."

Walking together, she realized Asa didn't have his cane with him and was holding onto her. It felt good that he leaned on her the slightest bit as they made their way back to the tables. She wanted to hurry, so that she could see where Katie was, but didn't want to rush. That would mean a separation from Asa. She needed him just as much as he needed her—to be close. When they reached the tables, the Bledsoes and Katie's family had cleaned up their baskets and everyone was on the lawn area playing games. Katie was not at the tables, not on the lawn areas, just as she feared.

"She's not here," Asa stated the obvious. "What's wrong?"

"I know. I was afraid of that." She sat on a bench, and he sat down next to her. Right next to her on the bench. She wanted to upbraid him about the inappropriate nature of this action in being so close to her, but she was too shaken.

"Should we go looking for her? Where do you think she is?"

"I know where she is." She told him about her experience standing in the ice cream line.

"Are you sure?"

"Katie has this…giggle." She struggled to bring the word forth. "Could they have sent those lawmen to come back here?"

"What? That's crazy."

"Is it? I can't even wrap my mind about what she would be doing with Paul Winslow behind that curtain. I don't even want to imagine it." She shook her head to rid herself of the mental pictures forming in her mind. "But those lawmen never, ever come in the back. They always stay up in the front. That's one of the reasons why we always grab a table back here." She looked up at Asa with her emotions reeling, her mind sifting through all of the things Katie knew. "Could she be some kind of a spy?"

Asa opened his mouth then shut it. She was looking at him for some answers, then she saw that Katie came up to her with a bowl of ice cream and held it out to her. Her hair didn't look as it usually did. "Hey Mags, this here for you."

She could see that the ice cream still had some semblance of a frozen appearance, and was not soupy yet. The sight of the slightly orange-colored ice cream made her stomach turn. Shaking her head no she turned away, unable to look at her friend.

"I would have brought some for you Mr. Thomas, but I didn't know you was back here with Mags. You all want to be alone?" And then she giggled. Mags's heart fell to the ground. Or it felt as if it did.

Asa took the ice cream bowl and placed it on the table between them. "You know what, that's an idea. We can share."

"Hmm. Hmm. I thought so. I'm going to see the three-legged races. Don't you all do anything I wouldn't do, now."

They both watched as Katie walked over to where the Negroes were engaged in vigorous games on the lawn side. Mags looked at the ice cream with a forlorn face. "I've never had ice cream that was so frozen before."

"Huh?" Asa picked up the spoon and dug in. "I was serious. Do you want to share?"

"Somehow, I think I'll never want ice cream again." She looked up at him. "This ice cream is a bribe."

"A bribe?"

"For my silence. I think she saw me there. Or maybe she saw me walking away. Once thing is for sure, Asa." She stilled his hand as he spooned the frozen treat into his mouth. "She's not trustworthy. We can't speak of things in front of her anymore. Not until I get to the bottom of this."

"You take care. If what you say is true, then we all are in danger." Asa put the spoon down, but her hand still rested on his. He squeezed it, stroking her knuckles with his thumb.

She might have protested, but right now, she needed some small comfort at the thoughts she was having.

She wished Independence Day were over.

There was a spy, Asa knew, but Katie? For Paul Winslow? Even as he thrilled to be sitting next to Mags and inhaling her sweet peachy scent, he kept an eye on Katie as she sat with her family. No. He could not imagine someone as vapid as Katie could be a spy at the mill.

Everyone came to the mill a little more tired the next day, since they had all been there for the fireworks the night before, so he drank a little extra coffee to stay alert. These were conditions ripe for someone getting mangled in the machines, an ever present concern.

At midday, Paul Winslow called him off of the floor into the office. "Yes, sir?"

Paul Winslow didn't invite him to sit down, a sure sign of trouble. Whatever the reason that he was being called in for, it was not a good one. "You seriously courting Mags Bledsoe?"

"Sir?" he asked. Did this mill owner have true investment in the comings and goings of Negroes? Interesting. When he lived in Pittsburgh, and traveling elsewhere, he thought white people cared nothing for the comings and goings of the Negroes.

"Don't be dense, Thomas. Are you courting her?"

He cleared his throat to give him more time. If Mags were going to stay, she had to work with this man after he had left and was long gone and he wanted to give the answer that would best position her for better work and hopefully, more responsibility. "I take my meals with the Bledsoes, sir, just like you told me."

"And you're staying there too."

"Now I am." Asa put it forward carefully, since he hadn't told Winslow directly he had rejected the mill house.

"Why don't you stay in the mill housing that I provided?"

If Katie were the spy, staying in the mill housing Winslow provided would allow him to see more of what was going on with Katie since his house was just across from theirs. Hmmm. A chill went up his spine at Mags's words. No. It couldn't be Katie.

"Someone, we never knew who, left a burning cross in front of my house, if you recall. I didn't feel welcome there. I thought it would be safer at the Bledsoes."

"Definitely more crowded," Paul Winslow offered up. "The mill house would have more room, and more privacy." He gave Asa a lewd smile. "A young buck like yourself would probably like to have a chance to be alone with his girl, wouldn't you?"

He fumed, but he kept his anger to himself. "Margaret Bledsoe is a good girl from a very respectable family. She has been an excellent employee here at this mill."

"True. However, I'm surprised at John. He's got all of those girls, all of them young and hot-blooded. Better to marry them off rather than letting them loose around town. It's dangerous."

His stomach turned at the sight of Paul Winslow's eyes. He tried to keep his tone light, but it was so hard. "I'm sure you didn't call me in to talk about who I might make Mrs. Thomas."

"Not if it concerns Mags Bledsoe."

"You just said she's just some young hot-blooded girl. What do you care about it?"

"I been hearing that you been taking her for rides in the car. Only one reason to go riding in the car—to court right?"

"Sure." Asa swallowed on the slight untruth. Still, if a lie protected Mags, he was willing to tell it.

"If you marry her, you'll want to take her on away from here, isn't that right?"

"If you're asking do I intend to return to Pittsburgh at the end of my assignment here, I do. I'm not interested in living here." He said this with a great deal of emphasis, knowing that what he said was truer now than ever. He did not like this man's unnatural interest in Mags, and now he could begin to see how Paul Winslow would not be above using someone as vapid as Katie to have her spy on her friend's comings and goings.

Tasting steel in his mouth, he knew he did not like that Mags was connected with this man. He resolved then and there to get her out of his grasp. Ruby was right after all. "Is that all?"

Paul Winslow was not satisfied with his answer. "Yes. Thank you, Thomas." Paul Winslow's jaw was tight, but too bad for it. He would get no more from him.

He went back out on the floor, and his gaze connected instantly with hers. She was doing her usual excellent work, but her face was open and questioning. Her beautiful black eyes and smooth brown skin made him feel very protective of her. So, he looked away.

In his view now, there was Katie, messing up the steps that he and Mags had taught her. So he went over to help her keep her work straight.

No one would harm Mags, not even her friend. Not on his watch.

"What did Paul Winslow say to you?" Mags practically attacked him with her words as soon as they were in the car alone after dropping Katie off at home.

"He wants me back in the mill house—wondered what was wrong."

"Did you tell him?"

"I did. I just wondered how he found out that I had moved into your parents' home."

"I know." She sat back in her seat and gave a grimace. "Katie must have told him."

He nodded his head slowly. "I have never seen a white man so interested in the comings, goings and dating life of a young Negro woman."

"What dating life?"

He better not try to deceive her. She could see he was reluctant to tell her but she did not care. "He wanted to know if you and I were courting. Officially."

"It's none of his business," Mags said with vigor. "How dare he ask you?"

"I guess he doesn't know that Ruby wants you to come up and help with the baby."

"No. He doesn't know because I don't see fit to tell him, and I never told Katie that I was sure."

"He's afraid you will leave him."

She quieted. She had been so busy trying to form complex plans that would make Paul Winslow suffer when the simplest solution was right in front of her eyes. She should go to Pittsburgh. Then he would suffer. But the mill would suffer too and the mill profits were the security for Adam, Solomon and Ruby's new baby. After all, Paul Winslow had to pass those assets along to someone. He had no one else.

"What did you tell him?"

"About what?"

Men. "If we were courting or not."

"I didn't tell him that. It's none of his business."

"I agree." It seemed their courting was no one's business, not even their own. She folded her hands as he pulled the car up to the front of the Bledsoe farm, where she saw that her father had the mules hitched up, ready to go somewhere. When Asa stopped the car, she got out.

"What is going on?" she called out to her father as he prepared to launch himself into the buckboard.

"Brother Carver and Sister Jane are coming in. I was going to get them from the train. I didn't know when you were coming."

"We could go get them, couldn't we?" She leaned down a little into the car to ask Asa. "The revival couple. They are coming into the train station to start revival next week."

"Of course."

She waved to her father and told him they would go. John waved back and she could see that he began to unhitch the mules.

"Thank you," Mags said, getting back into the car. "Daddy has long days in the summer keeping up with the farm, and a trip to town would be a burden just now, even though it is Brother Carver and Sister Jane. Reverend Forrest is very nice and everything, but Brother and Sister are our family's real spiritual guidance. We look forward to it when they come every summer, especially now because they couldn't come last year because of the flu."

"I'm fine with helping out."

"And if they ask, as I'm sure they will, you can tell them that we are not courting."

Ah. That shocked him. Good. She didn't want him thinking that she was just some simple country girl, pining away for his city slicker handsome self. "Whatever you want, Mags."

His cool tone made her blood boil. "We know that I'm not nearly good enough for you to court, so when you leave in a few more weeks, you can go back to Pittsburgh and find someone who is. Or maybe you can go back to France again."

She saw that his breath was measured. "I shared that with you because you told me about Travis and the fact that he died in your arms. I thought that it would matter to you that I had been through a similar kind of experience."

Mags shrugged her shoulders. "Why would it matter to me? And what was similar about it?"

"They were both people who were very dear to us and they died in our arms."

"Travis and I were a love unfulfilled. We were never able to get anywhere. He wanted to marry me. I was never sure of that with him. He was a farmer. I knew in helping my mother, I had enough of that kind of life. You, you were going to marry her."

"I had asked her."

"And she had accepted you. That makes it quite different from my situation."

"If that is the case, then why must you avenge his lynching?"

"Because he didn't deserve to die," Mags said heatedly, more than a little angered by his lack of understanding.

"And what made you think that Aline deserved to die? Because she was white?" Asa retorted.

The silence between them thickened and overwhelmed them both. No, it wouldn't be very difficult to let Brother Carver and Sister Jane know Mr. Thomas was no one who was any kind of potential husband to her. He had too much anger and love for another woman to ever make any room in his heart for another, let alone her.

Now she understood.

So why didn't she feel better?

Chapter Thirteen

Her heart rejoiced to see Brother Carver and Sister Jane. They were getting so old, that she was always afraid that one year they would say that they couldn't come, but here they were—two years after the last time. "Margaret, love. So good to see you," Sister Jane said, embracing her in her warm cushiony arms.

After they exchanged greeting, she took them over to the car. "We can drive you home in the car."

"That's a blessing. Who this?" Brother Carver asked with his friendly round face looking at Asa with curiosity.

"Asa Thomas. So good to meet you both." Mr. Thomas stepped and forward shook hands with both of them Mags noted and she made way for Brother Carver in the front.

"He's a vet from the war and came to the mill to supervise us."

"What? You still working in the mill? I never thought you would, honey…" Sister Jane's face was a puzzle.

Mags laughed. "Well, things change, just like the war changed things."

"For instance, she runs the mill." Asa slid into the front seat next to Brother Carver after he cranked up the car.

"Not really. Mr. Thomas came and took that job from me, so I'm back on the line. Just where a Negro woman belongs."

"Oh, I won't be staying here long. You can have your job back." Mr. Thomas's voice sounded light and far away.

"I'll be glad to have it back."

The Carvers seemed a bit shocked at the bickering that she engaged in with Asa. She knew the reprimand was coming, especially from Sister Jane who was never one to hold back her words. She would just wait for the right moment and after a silence, Sister Jane said, "This man isn't just your boss is he, honey?"

"Yes ma'am. He really is my boss."

"Ain't no way you be talking back smart to no boss man if you wants to keep your job. You gots a lot of emotion in your voice when you talking to him."

"Just things happening here. I'm fine. And so glad to see you, and the rest of the family will be as well." Mags squeezed her hand, but Sister Jane had a hound dog way about her.

"We be glad to see them too. We saw Ruby and the family just before we come. She's all round and pretty." Sister Jane's face reminded Mags of a nicely browned pie crust. She smiled at her. "I prays for her every night that she be all right."

"Mama'll want to hear every bit of what you say. She's been feeling so upset that she can't go up there and see to her herself, since Ruby has been having a hard time having babies with her husband."

"Do tell. So hard to know how things work in the Lord. She had Solomon so easy right off."

"Yes, but apparently, not with Adam."

"He done put her on bed rest. He's hired someone to be looking out for her and her little son 'til the baby come."

Mags felt a little chill. She should be with her sister, not some stranger. Maybe she should leave now, and go to give Adam and Ruby some relief. She could just stay for the revival and then maybe Brother and Sister could escort her up to Pittsburgh. That way, she could be taking care of more than one thing. She wouldn't have to be down here in Mr. Thomas's space all of the time and Paul Winslow would have to figure out what could be done without her. Both of them deserved one another.

They reached the Bledsoe farm and the whole family came out on the porch to greet them. Mags went inside quickly to see what could be done to help her mother, but she was chagrined to see everything was ready. Lona's face filled with delight and she seemed happier than she had been in a while.

"I want to hear all about Brother and Sister, so I got things done early. We can set down to eat."

Her mother had pulled together a special meal of fried beef steaks, potatoes and beans to go with the peach cobbler. She may have been weary of peaches, but Brother and Sister ate as if they couldn't get enough. When Lona and John heard that they had been up north and saw Ruby, they were ecstatic. When they had wrung every single detail out of Brother and Sister, Mags brought her plan forward as they lingered over coffee. "Since Ruby is on bedrest, then maybe I should go up sooner to relieve her. I can go on up with Brother and Sister if they'll have me."

The look of open hope had disappeared from her mother's face and instead, Lona's brows remained arched in a triangle on her face. She knew why. Ruby was on bedrest. Her mother would not want her there.

Sister Jane didn't seem to notice. "Bless your heart, child. You know that we would like nothing more than to go back up north with you, but after we leave here, we're going back south."

"Florida to see our son and his family. We be down there for a few months."

She tried her best to hide her disappointment. How could she get away from Asa? And Paul Winslow? "There's plenty bad going on here in Georgia and in other places," she spoke up.

"Lynchings. In the country. The cities." Brother folded his arms over his belly, satisfied with his peach cobbler.

"Our boys have come home, just like you Mr. Thomas, and they's asking for more changes. Whites don't like it."

"We came through here because we love you all, but we aim to get on away from here as soon as possible after the revival." Brother Carver shook his head. "Feels different here."

"Part of the reason that I'm here is to investigate these occurrences for the NAACP."

"Ruby let us know," Brother said. "I hope you find out things to help."

"I already have. Mags has been of invaluable help in my investigations," Mr Thomas said and she whipped her head at the sound of her name.

"Mighty glad to hear that," Sister Jane simpered. *Dear Lord.*

She stood to clear the table. Sister would want to hear every little detail and that newspaperman would oblige her.

Mags stayed in the kitchen and cleaned. She cleaned all of the dinner dishes, pans and pots and began to get an early start on cooking the tongue for tomorrow afternoon's sandwiches. Nothing of a butchered calf went to waste around here. She startled when Mr. Thomas approached her to come back to the room off of the kitchen. He was giving it up to the Carvers despite their protests that they could stay in the barn. "Gotta clear a few things out so that Brother and Sister will be more comfortable in here."

"You could go back to your mill house. To satisfy Paul Winslow. See what Katie is up to."

"I'm going to stay out on the porch. Your father has a cot and it is warm enough."

She bit her lips, not liking the thought of Asa on the big porch just outside her window. Still, it was something that happened from time to time in their capacity as borders for Negroes in Winslow. "Whatever satisfies you."

He stopped and regarded her. "You've been a big help. We could make one more trip before I leave."

"You could be better alone. We don't seem to get along that well." She averted her eyes. Maybe they got along too well.

"Anything that happened is my fault."

"No, I just, I think that we come from different worlds. That's all."

"You sure that's it? That you aren't afraid?"

Of course I'm afraid. She shook her head.

"We're doing a great work. I need your assistance. Please."

"I'll think about it." *If you would just leave me alone.*

"You cannot leave without me, Mags." He moved closer to her in the hot kitchen.

She stepped away from the stove and now, she looked him squarely in the face. "You might be the big boss man at work, but you don't boss me anywhere else."

He moved right along with her, almost as if they were in a dance. "I do care for you, Mags. You know that, right?"

No one was more than stunned than she when he reached an arm out, wrapped it around her waist and pulled her close to him, kissing her full on the mouth once again.

He didn't drink. His mother brought him up as temperance. Still, when he was kissing Mags, he sipped on the finest liquor and his head spun at her sweet taste and the juiciness of her lips. Then, when he thought it couldn't get any better, he realized that she was kissing him back and the melding together of their mouths sent his mind to reeling.

"Oh, Mags, you is kissing him!" Delie shouted out the words by the kitchen door.

They instantly broke apart and Asa turned around to see the entire cohort of the Bledsoes, along with Sister Jane and Brother Carver, clustered in the doorway.

She stepped apart from him and poked at something in her cooking pot. He didn't know whether to admire her or to feel insulted at her cool under their scrutiny. The unruffled Mags said, "The proper verb, Cordelia May, is are. You are kissing him."

Delie had the good grace to look ashamed, while her two younger sisters giggled. Since there was nothing to see, the family started slipping away from the doorway and he heard Brother Carver laughing and saying to John Bledsoe, "Look like you better be asking his man what his intentions are, Johnny."

His heart plummeted to his stomach and he stepped forward to Lona, whose eyes looked just like Ruby's when she threw his cane at him. "I apologize. I'll leave and stay in the mill house."

John looked sympathetic since he already knew what his intentions were.

However, Lona was not. "I'ma have you to know no one ever come up into this house—God's house—with the intentions getting at one of my daughters like a fox in the hen house. We trying to raise our girls proper here."

Her angered tone reminded him about his potential inadequacies as a husband for Mags and he ducked into the room to gather his things to leave.

Mags stepped forward. "Mama, I believe that I have some say in this."

"You most certainly do not. I have never been so scandalized in all of my life."

Mags confronted her mother. "I seem to recall Ruby having her share of encounters with Adam."

"They may have had some times together, but it was not up under our roof, I'll have you to know missy." Lona sputtered as Sister Jane grabbed her mother by the shoulders.

"Calm down, Lona. There's be plenty of us to see to the young people while we are here. We can make sure they stay respectable, right?" Jane nodded at the two of them, and guided her mother out of the doorway.

The small kitchen slowly emptied out until it was just Delie standing in the kitchen looking at them. "Get out of here," Mags hissed at her little sister.

"No way. I'm staying to get me some lessons."

Mags chased after her with a kitchen towel and Delie left the kitchen until the two of them were again by themselves, door wide open. Mags stood in the doorway, slightly winded from chasing her young sister around. "I think you owe me an explanation, Mr. Thomas."

"For what?"

"For why you keep doing that."

"Kissing?" Asa spread his hands. "Why does a man kiss a woman? To know how her lips taste. To be close to her. To let her know that he cares."

"To marry her," she said. Silence from him. "Yes, that is what I thought. You're just down here to have a good time. You would marry a white woman, but you're down here to have a good time with me."

"That's not true. And I don't call writing about Negro men being lynched as fun."

"Okay. I mean in between the reporting. You're having a good time."

He folded his arms. "Well, yes. Aren't you?"

"No." The sound of her no weighted heavy on his heart. "You confuse me. As someone who knows her mind all of the time, you've come in here and messed that up and I don't like it."

"What do you want me to say, Mags? I'm sorry."

"That's a start. But I also want to know what your intentions are with me."

Asa spread his hands again. "You're intelligent, beautiful and charming. You have been very helpful to me in my investigation. The time we have spent together has been a wonderful balm to my heart. Any man would be lucky to have you as his bride."

"But not yours."

He would endure the pain of being shot all over again, rather than hurt her. "I cannot." He made a helpless gesture. "Forgive me, God, but I cannot."

"Cannot, or will not?"

"I cannot. I'm sorry."

"Maybe it's my forgiveness you should seek. When it is time for you to leave, you can go back up north and find some other, lighter woman who will suit you." She untied her apron and he reached out to grab her arm.

"That's not it. Please, Mags, believe me."

"Then what is it?"

Asa cleared his throat. "You deserve better than me, Mags, don't you see it? Your mother even said it. I don't mean to take advantage of you, but there is some man out here who can be the man you deserve."

"Why don't I deserve someone like you?" The truthfulness in her question and in her eyes caused his heart piece as if wounded.

"Mags, please. Just know that whatever I do, I did it so that you can find happiness elsewhere." *That didn't come out right. Please God, help me explain it to her.*

"You have a funny way of showing it." Mags crinkled her nose and the skin on her smooth brown forehead winkled too. *God, she is adorable.*

"Maybe, but it is what I intended."

"You're a cad."

"Far from it."

"Well, that is what I'll tell Ruby when I get to her. I'll let her know what a cad you are, going around and trifling with young country girls and their feelings. I hope that your mother and sisters are proud." She shook herself free of his hold, walked out of the kitchen.

The very air holding him up left him.

Watching her walk out of the room, tall and able to escape his hold, he was sorry he had ever said anything to that white officer. If he hadn't said anything, he would have a whole leg. He would have been able to court Mags, propose to her and be a full husband to her.

Instead, he could do none of that and now Mags hated him.

Some of the feeling he had in his room at his mother's house crept in at the edge of his consciousness.

Mags went through the front room, sweeping past her family and the Carvers and into her room, seeking the comfort of her Bible. She opened it to her favorite place. She liked to read of the sacrifices that her namesake, Ruth, had made in following her mother-in-law's people and how Ruth's courage had led to the founding of Israel.

Could she be a vessel like that one day? No. Instead, she was relegated to staying in her father's house and serving him and her mother all of the days of her life. She lay down on the bed and felt hot tears soak into the pillow as she rested and fell asleep.

She must have been really tired, because when she woke up there was morning light peering into the windows and it was time to get Sunday breakfast ready. She woke up and tiptoed through the front room and across to the kitchen and lit the stove to get ready for another day. Surviving, going on, that was her specialty.

She sat at one end of a pew during the church service and Mr. Thomas sat at another. She did not seek out his company for the rest of the day. When he said he was going to the mill house to write for a bit, she shrugged her shoulders and acted as if she didn't care. She couldn't help but stare after him as he drove away.

"Where's he going?" John stepped up to her as she swept the front yard.

"He says he is going to write at the mill house. He'll be back for supper."

"Do you care for him, daughter?"

Mags swept harder. "He was just someone different to come into our lives. Soon, he'll leave and go back to his home and all will be as it was before."

"Do you believe all that?"

"Mostly." She leaned on her broom. "I'm just looking for things to be as they were before he came."

John shook his head. "God put him into our lives for a reason. We're made different by his light. We're changed now and we can't ignore that."

"I can."

"It don't do to deny that you care for him."

"He denies it about me." She kept up her sweeping furiously, trying not to have her pain at his rejection of her manifest itself into tears.

"Daughter. He still trying to cope with the loss of his leg. He feels like he can't be no man or husband to you without it. He still trying to find his way. Be patient."

"Did he say that to you?"

"Something like. He cares a great deal for you."

"I would like to believe that. His leg doesn't matter to me."

"It matter to him, and that matters. Your mama didn't help none when she said what she did."

Her mother was such a cross to bear in more ways than one. She kept her anger down as she thought of the commandment that her father had reminded her of. "It doesn't matter, Daddy."

"I'm telling you. Just be loyal and steadfast."

She swallowed her anger and felt chagrined. She chased Asa away when she should have stood by him. "I guess I'll let him know I'm sorry when he gets back."

"Don't say nothing to him directly about it. Be Margaret Ruth and be steadfast. I bet he'll come around, feeling better about his leg, and himself. We take it to the revival tomorrow and lift it up to the Lord."

She inhaled and breathed out. Yes, the thought of the revival tomorrow made her feel much better and much stronger. She could lift it up to God.

Help Asa in the way that he felt about the loss of his leg.

Help me to remain steadfast.

Please God, let the cloud lift in his heart and make room for me there.

For the first time in a long time, she prayed with all her heart in it.

Because she was in love with him.

Chapter Fourteen

Mags loved the music at the revival the most. She wished she could sing, really express herself to God that way, but she didn't have the talent so all she could do was hum the country hymns inaccurately.

Sometimes, her younger sisters would sing in harmony and her eyes would smart with tears to hear those youngsters sing. She hoped they were working on something to sing for the Carvers. Nettie, especially, had the voice of an angel. Her wide eyes gave her an ethereal appearance that, when people saw her, made them respect her just that little bit more. Paul Winslow, for instance, didn't mess with Nettie. Still, Nettie wasn't doing as well with her high school studies. What would become of her without an education?

"Focus. Make sure that you focus," Asa reprimanded her as he passed. He didn't sound as if he cared for her more than any other worker, it was just his job. Or was it hers? She was so confused, she didn't know what to think about it anymore. Asa Thomas or was it Asa Caldwell? Whoever he was confused her and she just wanted him to go away. His last day couldn't come soon enough.

"You sure are quiet, Mags," Katie said to her as Asa drove them home in the car that afternoon. Paul Winslow always let them have off two hours early on revival nights.

"Got my mind on the revival."

"I would come out with you all," Katie said, "but Mama and Daddy'll ride in from town, so I'ma see you all there."

Katie smelled of some weird perfume. Mags turned her head to look out of the window, in order to smell the outdoors and not the heavy floral scent her friend reeked of. On top of that, she knew Katie didn't have the money to buy those kind of extras. Just like Mags, her earnings went to help her family and there wasn't enough for pretty perfume. Did Paul Winslow give it to her?

When Katie left the car, she had to hold herself back from asking Asa to drive faster just so that heavy, lingering smell could evaporate from the car. She didn't really want to talk to him.

"I want to apologize for the way things went on Saturday," Asa said to her after clearing his throat. They were the only ones in the car.

"That's fine." She looked out of the window.

"I'm going to be here another two weeks and I really think that we should make peace so that these rides are not unbearable for us."

Mags turned to him. "They're not unbearable for me. I'm fine. I don't need to hear all of your boss talk from the mill. I can sit here and just enjoy the ride. Or, better yet, I can walk, just as I used to before you came. I don't need you to drive me around."

"I know you spend a lot of energy at the mill, and it's good to help you save strength for your legs for when you have to work hard at home."

The way that he said it made it sound so nice and thoughtful, just as if he really cared for her. She was taken in for a second, but only a second. *He doesn't really care, he's just pretending.*

Then, it hit her with a blinding force.

He had concern for her legs. He, who didn't have two good legs, as she did, cared for her legs. *How could I be so selfish?* "My legs?" she asked, nearly choking with emotion as he pulled up into her parents' front yard. "They are just fine. Thank you for your concern about me."

She turned to him. "How is your leg?"

He started at her question. "I have pain from time to time. It really was something getting used to this new leg. But I have been. And now, it isn't as bad."

"That's good. It's attached to you by…"

"My hips. I wear the attachment around my hips and there are leather straps that go down my thigh to the leg."

"I see." Her eyes were drawn to the area that he was talking about, even as she knew it was rude. How did it all work? Was it efficient for him?

"I can't show you, Mags. It wouldn't be decent." Asa smiled at her. "Unless we were mar—"

He stopped at the word and she nodded her head. Opening the car door to leave, she said, "Married? Yes. And we know that could never happen. I better get inside to fix dinner before the revival."

"Yes, I guess so. Thank you."

What was he thanking her for? And really, she had behaved shamefully just now. She should be the one to apologize, except she remembered so clearly with the sharpness of the tip of a knife, his rejection of her.

She would treat him as a brother in Christian love until it was time for him, and perhaps her, to go up north and they would part company forever.

She smoothed over the pang in her heart by adjusting her dress, readying it for her work apron.

How could it be painful by watching someone move in the world? It was. He remembered their brief kisses as if it were the most precious liqueur—fated to never have any more. All he could do was watch her from afar, aching, always aching to touch her, never being allowed to.

He could be proud of her. Thinking of her movements in the house, he knew she would be extremely efficient about preparing the meal and making everything comfortable in the crowded Bledsoe house before the revival.

He was going to go. Many Negroes as well as whites would be there to attend the prayer meetings. You never knew what might be there to help with the investigation.

Maybe he could ask God to help him deal with this pain in his heart at hurting her.

She constantly amazed him. She had never asked questions about his leg. No one had. They rather acted as if his leg pain would go away, or if as if it were just fine. But it wasn't. Or was it? He shook his head, thinking of her concerned eyes as she looked at him and asked questions about his leg. Her concerned eyes were something that was much better to view, in his opinion, than her distant, angry ones.

Dinner was a quick affair, but an appropriate cold plate with chicken and salads. Asa offered to take the Carvers to the revival tent in the car, and they accepted. "But only if Mags comes along," Sister Jane said. "Ruby used to help us set up, but Mags can take it on."

"I usually walk with my sisters, but if you feel that you need me, and Mr. Thomas doesn't mind, then I'll be glad to come."

"Absolutely," he said as he watched her take off her apron. She had changed into a lighter colored skirt with a shirtwaist that was a little lacy. It looked like some of the material from the mill and he asked her if that was where it came from.

"Yes, it is. Em is a whiz with a needle. She does all of our clothes."

Yes, Em was the reason sisters were all so well turned out and now he knew. He nodded to Em and he noticed that the young woman blushed under his praise. She had a darker skin, but looked a lot like Lona, and she had freckles just like Ruby.

He went out to the car and the Carvers followed. The drive to the revival tent was not far. The tent stood proud and tall in Paul Winslow's vast back yard that bordered the far edge of John Bledsoe's farm. The early hours off and keeping the tent on his land were more examples of Paul Winslow's largesse, Asa noted. *How kind of him.* The revival Mags had told him, was the one religious event where the entire Winslow community worshipped God together. Every Sunday, everyone went to their respective churches, isolated, races separate.

He pulled up to the revival tent and helped the Carvers unload their table dressings from the car. Some families had already come and everyone had brought various blankets or chairs to sit on which made it rather festive.

Mags orchestrated, in her usual efficient way, helping the Carvers set up the front part of the tent for the services, and the set of her shoulders proved she didn't care about his very existence.

So, he was free to speak to some of the early arrivals whom he did not know. Most of them, once Mags had given the okay, let him know that they had been witness to a tightening of the rules and regulations in their communities. He read this as some of the landowners trying to prevent more lynching, but those restrictions would just make things worse.

He turned as he heard the first sweet notes of a harmonica sound, and saw Sister Jane was playing a lively tune. While he admired her musicianship, he saw the two law enforcement officials from the Independence Day celebration stood at the back of the tent. He could tell that, once again, their presence was a surprise because as people saw them, they stopped clapping in time to Sister Jane's music and pointed and whispered. Sister Jane saw they were there, but she did not stop playing. Brother Carver kept an eye on them and he kept slapping his pant leg in time to the music.

Good for them.

They were willing to accept the presence of a snake in the tent. Still, it angered him that the Negroes in this town couldn't worship as they pleased without the police presence there. Brother Carver stepped forward and spread his arms wide. "Welcome in the name of Jesus, brothers and sisters!"

"Amen!" the crowd chanted back to him as if they were part of some previously rehearsed chorus.

"We are so happy to be back, praise Jesus. However, we want to make sure that tonight, and all of the nights of the revival are dedicated in the Lord for those who have gone on before us because of that influenza last year, Amen." Everyone lowered their heads to pray, as did Asa.

The picture of Aline came to him again, and this time, he was slightly surprised. He could barely remember her face. He remembered her honey-colored hair. He remembered that she had dainty hands, but that they were rough-hewn on the inside because of her hard work in her parents' bistro. She liked to wear yellow. But her face, the features of her face blurred in his memory. He wished he had a photograph of her. She deserved to be remembered, but he didn't know how.

He lifted his head when Sister Jane spoke.

"We going to have lots of music tonight, and we going to start with the Bledsoe sisters. Come on girls." Sister Jane invited and Nettie, Em and Delie all stood up in front of the crowd without the least bit of fear or trepidation. When the girls opened their mouths to sing in harmony, it created a sweet sound that touched the hearts of the audience. Several people dabbed at their eyes at the rendition of "Rock of Ages" and he himself felt a certain pride at Margaret's tall, slim sisters singing at the front of the crowd.

One of the lawmen cleared his throat when they sat down after their song. Why didn't they just let the people worship? This was a basic American right.

Still, as Sister Jane promised, the revival was a lot of music interspersed with people who stood up to give a testimony about a loss in their lives. Asa sat on a chair in the back and put his leg out to rest it. He didn't want to always take notes, but he also didn't want to get involved in all of the emotional aspects of the testimonial parts, even as he enjoyed the music.

Brother Carver was looking at him, he could tell, but he didn't look back. He was determined to keep the reporter's prospective, and take notes in his notebook, much to the displeasure of the lawmen.

He noticed that the lawmen were there again on Tuesday and Wednesday night. "You would think," he said to John, "that they noticed this is a peaceful gathering of people who just want to worship. Wasn't that all what the founding of America was about?"

John chimed in, "That's what they say. But there's a mighty lot going on just now, and men like Paul Winslow are bound and determined to protect their property. That's why them lawmen are there."

By Wednesday, those lawmen were so comfortable, they brought their own chairs to sit down in and they sometimes clapped along with the music. Every time they did, he balled up his fists. His hands would loosen, though, as Sister Jane nodded at them, passing by them as if they were everyone else.

"Judge not, lest ye be judged," Sister Jane said after she had finished playing another hymn on the harmonica. "People are being changed here tonight, friends. Hearts are being changed right before our eyes. This is what our meetings are about. Sometimes, people feel a little closer to God out here in his temple of nature, Amen."

"Amen," several people echoed her.

Brother Carver jumped up faster than Asa thought he could. "We need another testimony. We need someone who will open their hearts here amongst us. Some of us have heavy hearts, Lord. We need to talk about what we have lost. We need to share ourselves, Lord, so that you know that we are not alone, but that you are with us, Amen."

Asa knew that Brother Carver wanted him to speak. He had avoided his pleading so far, but he figured that he might as well get it over with. Asa put his cane forward, leaned on it and stood up. "I want to offer a testimony."

Brother Carver's face was wreathed in smiles. "Amen, Brother Asa. Here we have a very wonderful special guest in our midst who will be leaving you all not long after we do. Please, Brother, come forward and speak in the name of God."

Asa stood up next to Brother Carver and looked around at the expectant faces. What could he possibly offer? Then, the comforting, smooth brown face of Mags came into his view. She sat there, as regal and confident as a queen, ready to hear what he had to say. Her eyes held no judgment. She gave him the strength to speak and he started. "I didn't want to fight a war without knowing what it was about. Some terrible things were happening in Europe, but I didn't want to kill my fellow man without knowing why. I went over there to find out, and to see how I could help."

Some of what he was saying made for some talk amongst the racially mixed audience. He knew that all of them believed in fighting for America, but he did not want to lie to God. "I signed up, going to help shed light on the way that the Negro troops were suffering. They were not being treated fairly by the military, and I knew that I had talents that could help them, more than the letters they wrote home to their families."

He didn't say that he was a journalist. That would be the red meat that those lawmen in the back wanted, and he noticed the lawmen stood up out of their chairs to hear his testimony. "However, when I got there, I was persecuted for asking questions. I lost my leg, not because I was in the wrong place at the wrong time on the battlefield. That would be a wonderful story. I lost it because of hate. Another man hated that I asked questions and he shot me there, on purpose. Twice." Gasps of shock rose from the crowd and Em whipped out a handkerchief. He gave her a comforting look to show the young girl he was okay. She dabbed at her eyes and put it away.

Mags's jewel eyes willed him on to tell his story. "I knew that I was there for God's purpose, on God's work, and I shouldn't feel anger because of my lost leg. But I did. I was angry at God for a long time because of my leg."

Everyone was quiet. "I turned my back on God. I doubted that he had anything in mind for me. There were times when I was healing that I wanted to take everything that God had given me and just, just, tell him to leave me alone. That I did not deserve to continue in this life."

Asa barely heard some of the shocked gasps. "It has taken me a long time to see that God didn't leave me. He has been here with me all along. He's protecting me and guiding me as I do his work. God's work for me is to keep asking questions. I'm going to keep doing that, as long as He shows me he has a plan for me and that I have a purpose in this world. Amen."

No one said anything as he walked back to his chair in the back and sat down. When he did, he was surprised to notice that his face was drenched with sweat. He took out a handkerchief and wiped his face down.

The lawmen sat back down as he did and that they did not seem to like his testimony that much. Good. He never again intended to bow down to some man's will just because they didn't like the color of his skin.

Some people shouted things out and his testimony motivated others to move forward and receive blessings from Brother Carver. Seeing them be blessed made him happy, even as he didn't yet feel the relief that he sought. What would it take for the burden to be lifted from him?

Katie was one of the ones who made her way forward to receive Brother

Carver's blessing. The girl sobbed and wept profusely. "Clean me. Help me to be clean in Jesus's name." Katie wept.

Brother Carver laid his hands on her to try to give her some peace, and Sister Jane stepped forward to help hold her, but Katie writhed around on the ground, moaning and shaking. "Receive the blessing of God, Sister," Brother Carver said, but it seemed to do Katie no good.

"I've been so bad, please Jesus," Katie sobbed.

"We all have, honey. Take his blessing." Sister Jane soothed her, but Asa could tell that they wanted her to sit down so that they could move on to the next part of the meeting. Katie's sorrow and sobs were so deep that she couldn't let them. Would Mags get up to help her friend? No. She sat there watching.

"I been fornicating, Jesus, and I needs forgiveness."

Brother Carver was shocked but he kept on blessing poor Katie.

Mags was right. He looked over at her and her eyes met his. How would he let her know that she was right and he should have listened to her?

Katie blubbered on. "I got a baby in me, God, and I don't know what to do."

Mags stood then and moved forward to help Katie away. However, she was not the only one. The lawmen came forward and shoved Mags to the side to get to Katie before Mags could.

Asa was up on his cane and at Mags's side to help her up. "I'm fine. Help Katie."

Everyone watched as the lawmen each took one of Katie's arms and dragged her up the aisle, kicking and screaming.

The lawmen ignored the shouted protests of Brother Carver and Sister Jane as they boldly hauled Katie away. However, they went down the wrong aisle. Asa followed them as fast as he could, shouting, "Where are you taking her? This is a worship, and she should not be hauled away."

"Mind your own business. This girl is causing a public disturbance"

"I cannot let you do that in God's house."

They stopped because Katie quieted and the sheriff threw her arm off in the red dirt. "See, she's quiet now. Let the service go on."

"I don't like you, boy," the sheriff growled. "You been getting into business that you shouldn't be getting into."

Asa caught up to the two lawmen, helping Katie to her feet. "If someone is coming into God's house and trying to arrest someone, that makes it my business, and I'm going to say something about it."

"Move out of my way 'fore I shoot your other leg. Then you won't have any good leg to stand on."

That struck the sheriff as funny and he and his friend laughed.

All of Asa's anger charged up his arms and he reacted in the way he should have when the sergeant shot off his leg.

He reached out and punched the sheriff right on the jaw.

Chapter Fifteen

Forever after, Mags always regretted that she didn't stand to help Katie when she first started babbling. She could clearly see that the Carvers were a bit stunned by Katie's ensuing revelations and Margaret was her friend, or at least she thought she was.

She was too angry at Katie's betrayal and had sought to stay away from her for as long as possible. She felt pride—that terrible sin—at the fact that she had kept away from Katie when she admitted in front of God and the revival crowd that she had been impure. Her sinning, willingly, with Paul Winslow had resulted in a baby. It all seemed to be too much to take in.

She should have felt compassion. She had hoped people would feel the same toward her sister when she had been attacked and had a child. People didn't. They judged. And now, when her supposed friend had fallen in the same desperate way as Ruby, she stood back and judged.

Because of her pride and judgment, chaos ensued at the revival.

First, when those lawmen came forward and started dragging Katie off, that confirmed everything she suspected. Katie was in the pay of Paul Winslow. She had been his lover and had betrayed Mags. When her friend was dragged off, she didn't feel compelled to stop it—she felt pride that her friend should be publicly humiliated.

Her stomach twisted into a knot when Asa confronted those men. They had guns. That was when she stood. She knew that she loved him and didn't want him to come to a bad turn. He stood his ground and Mags was shocked to see his attack on the sheriff. Secretly, she was thrilled, because someone should have attacked Winslow's sheriff years ago, but at the same time she was horrified because Asa was putting his life into deep, deep jeopardy. Men had been lynched for far less.

"Asa!" she shouted and in the scuffle, several gunshots went off. The fear of the crowd increased and all of a sudden, crowds of people came between her and Asa and she clawed and fought her way to get back to him. She had to see if he was hurt. Since she was tall, Asa was about to find her and fought his way to her through the panicked crowd that rushed out of the tent.

"Are you alright?" she said, but even when it was halfway out of her mouth, she could see that he was. *Thank you God.*

"We've got to get out of here," Asa shouted above the loud horrified roars of the people. He grasped her hand and she briefly reveled in its warmth and strength.

Her heart jump started when she thought of her family. She turned around and was relieved to see her sisters heading for the side of the tent and her mother and father following them, her father shielding her mother. Thank God. They were alright.

Asa and Mags headed up front to where the Carvers were standing, the only ones not panicked.

"We've got to get out," Asa repeated to them and she could see the reluctance of Brother Carver and Sister Jane to leave.

"Someone done been shot back there," Brother Carver craned his neck to see.

"It's Katie. They shot her," Asa said. "We've got to get out. There's nothing more that can be done for her."

Something evil twisted inside of her at this revelation. Her friend was dead? Gone? How had things turned upside down so quickly? All at once, she saw the one lawman heading for them, trying to get to Asa through the crowd. She grabbed at Sister Jane's hand with her other free hand and pulled. They followed him through the crowd and went outside to where the car was. He started the car and gestured to her. She hopped into the passenger side of the car.

John Bledsoe came up to them with a panicked expression. "You got to get out of this county, the law will be after you."

"I'm not afraid," Asa said resolutely.

"They'll kill you," Mags shouted. "They'll lynch you."

"Guess I'll have the inside story then."

"Go!" John smacked the car and Asa pulled the car off.

She knew she shouldn't but she needed to see where those horrible lawmen were. The crowd had surrounded the car and the deputies weren't able to get out as quickly as they might have wanted to. They both struggled to get into their car in order to chase Mags and Asa down. "Leave the car at the house, so Paul Winslow can get it. You don't need to owe him a thing," Mags directed. "We can hide in the woods. I'll show you where."

"You'll stay at the house. I'll hide in the woods."

"I'm coming with you, Asa. You cannot stop me from coming with you," Mags looked at him. "I owe you." She wanted to say, I love you, but she didn't know how he would take it.

Thank God the crowd had given them a head start. Those fool lawmen would have made it faster down here if they just ran, but they were too stupid to realize. She ran into the kitchen and packed a rucksack full of cold biscuits and some leftover sweet potatoes. She ran back out to Asa. "We have to go on foot."

"I can do it. Let's go."

Getting to the pond was a much tougher job in the dark than when they went fishing in the first of the morning. However, she had gone there so often, she knew the way. They could stay at the old parsonage, where Reverend Dodge used to live, before the new pastor had come and wanted something better for his wife and family in town.

The inside of the parsonage was very dark, but she knew where the church's stores of kerosene were kept. She retrieved a lamp and brought it back to the parsonage where Asa waited. She put the lamp down in a corner and laid a small blanket on the floor.

Asa had retrieved some wood from the woodpile and tried to start a fire in the fireplace. She took some of the kerosene to help him and soon, there was a fire in the fireplace. Maybe it wasn't a necessity in July, but it made her feel better. Asa sat himself on the blanket and she sat beside him. Now that they were able to stop and breathe, all of her sensible aspect went away from her and she shook uncontrollably at what had just happened.

Asa attacked the sheriff. Even if he had pushed on him, Paul Winslow and his henchmen would not stop until they came to get him.

"Stop. Look, I need to tell you some things before they come for me. I want you to go home where it is safe," Asa said in a calm voice, reaching over to pull her to him. Her trembling in this terrifying moment allowed her into his arms willingly.

"Mags, you know that they'll come for me. I don't want you to be here when they do. I wanted to tell you that my notebook with all of my research is under the front seat of the car. I want you to get it and take it up north to Ruby. Now, today, as soon as you possibly can. The investigation notes need to stay safe. This thing is bigger than me, and we've got to make sure that other people know what is going on down here."

She held on to his boiled shirt just a little bit more. She was happy to feel his broad chest against hers, and their hearts beating in time together. He felt so safe and secure. She didn't want to give up this feeling for anything. Pulling back, she touched his face. He touched her cheek as well and she put her lips to his and they kissed, freely, holding nothing back. They were kissing each other desperately, as if it were their last kiss, which it might have been.

When they parted, he grabbed her shoulders, and gave her a sad half-smile. "You probably should leave now Mags. You'll be in bigger danger if you stay here in my arms than in facing some lynch mob."

Mags wanted to shout at him for joking and that she didn't care. She could give herself to him right there on Dodge's unswept floor if he would have her. Then, she took her own shaky breath and realized what he was saying was wise. She was endangering her own life, as well as her virtue, if she stayed with him.

"The first train out doesn't leave for a few hours. At about seven in the morning."

"That's fine. Go to the mill house until the train comes. I'm afraid that they'll be after your family until they know where I am and then they'll be after you."

He was right. Taking in a horrified breath she realized that her family was vulnerable to questioning. She had to get back to the farm to make sure that they were all right. Asa drew a key out from his pocket and handed it to her. As he did, his pant leg hitched up and she could see the false leg, just a little bit. He could see that she could see his leg and he made a move to grasp his knife sharp cuff and pull the pant leg down a bit. Mags touched his hand and stayed it.

"No, don't," she said. "Let me see it."

He started to open his mouth in protest, but then he let go of the cuff. Mags traced her hand down cuff to the edge of the pant and kneeling in front of the leg, she slowly lifted the pant leg up, surprised to see that the fake leg was brown, and almost matched Asa's skin tone. It was not wooden as she thought.

"It is made of something called Bakelite. It's thought to have more give than wood."

She continued to pull his pant leg up and saw where the Bakelite leg ended and where the stump of his real leg began, wrapped in bandages. "Do the bandages keep it from hurting?"

"That's what they are meant to do. It doesn't always work that well." He smiled ruefully.

She touched the bandaged part of his leg, and she heard him take in his breath sharply. "I'm sorry," she said quickly. "I don't want to hurt you."

"It doesn't hurt. Not anymore. It is just that...no one has ever touched it before."

"No one?"

"Besides doctors."

"Not even your mother or sisters?"

Asa smiled and his eyes betrayed a sadness there that she had not seen before. "My mother would rather pretend that I'm whole and that there's nothing wrong with my leg. What she does, my sisters do."

Mags touched the bandaged part again and stroked it lovingly. She patted it and pulled his pants leg down again over the leg. She sat back on her haunches and looked at him in the dim light. "You don't have anything to be ashamed of."

She could see that he was about to deny that he was ashamed. But he couldn't. "I'm not a whole man, Mags. Forget me."

She took him by the shoulders. "I'm never ever, ever going to abandon you. Not because of your leg. Not for anything. I want to stay with you."

"I won't have it. You must be safe."

"They got to Travis. I won't let them take someone that I love again." Asa put a hand on her arm and drew her closer to him once more. They kissed again and he could feel her tremble as she pulled back from him.

"Your lips are so sweet," Asa said. "If I could, I would kiss you over and over again."

"And you'll have the chance to." She stood up on her shaky legs. "Once we're married."

"I cannot marry you. You need a whole man who will take care of you."

"I can take care of me. You avenged me and Katie tonight. That has to count for something." His face was a puzzle, mulling it all over. Once again, she was purposeful. "I'm going to go into town and get train tickets for us."

"Leave mine at the train window. I don't know if I'll ever use it."

"No!" Mags knelt down and kissed him again. "You will because I say it. We must pray to God." She stopped and bowed her head. When she looked up, she could see that Asa was looking at her, not praying.

"How can I go wrong with such a precious Pearl praying for me?"

Mags lowered her head. "I have to confess that I do like that name better."

"Then it's what I'll call you, from now on. And no more Mr. Thomas from you."

"I love you, Asa," Mags said, and she was surprised at how easily it came to her lips now when their lives were on the line.

"And I love you, my Pearl. Now go and stay safe. See that the research notes are kept safe."

"I will." She slipped out into the night away from his warmth. Hearing nothing, she started back through the woods to the farm, feeling hot tears slip down her cheeks. *God, please, please, please keep him safe. It isn't fair that something should happen to him, and to love for me now, once again, once it is so close. Please look out for us. Please.*

A glow reached her through the woods, as she got closer to the farm. Had God heard her prayer? Maybe it was too late. With her heart pounding, she peered through the trees, and saw them. Night riders. In the front yard of the peaceful Bledsoe farm, they burned a cross in the clear front yard of her beloved family's farm.

Asa was filled with fear, not for the lynch mob to come, but over Mags. Was it right to tell her to go back into the woods to her family? They may have caught up with her there.

Time went by, and he even was able to nap a little, but no one came. His dreams were full of visions of dogs hunting him down and a lynch mob coming to get him. Still, when none of those things happened, rather than feeling secure in his safety, he felt fear.

Within a few hours though, that felt like days, he determined the best course of action was to turn himself in. No more fear like this. It was too much tension. He would rather just hand himself over and face his punishment, whatever it would be.

And he felt better about it now than he felt when he was in bed, ready to use the contraband gun on himself. He had lived and he had helped a worthy young lady to learn about love. He had left a legacy and Mags would see to it his reporting would reach the world.

Emerging from the parsonage, he ate some of the food that Mags had bought in the rucksack and stored it up on a high shelf where it was before. Pulling up his suspenders, he went in search of some fresh water to drink from the creek. The freshness of the water made him feel revitalized, and he splashed some on his face when the sound of a car engine reached him.

His first inclination was to run, but he knew that he wasn't going to go anywhere. He was ready to face his punishment. He stood and turned to face the oncoming car. It was Bob, the chauffeur for the Winslows, and Paul Winslow was in the back of the car.

"I was worried about you. 'Fraid you might not report to work this morning." Paul Winslow alighted from the car, settling his bulk just so.

"I'm fine."

"Said you caused a bit of a ruckus at the revival last night. I said, I couldn't believe that my manager would do that. He's a good one, he is, but no, they said it was you what attacked an officer of the law and then ran off."

"I did it," he said not sure if this confession would incriminate him. He didn't care.

"That's a shame," Paul Winslow nodded his head. "We had worked so well together. Well. Clearly, you cannot stay around here. I cannot have Negroes of any stripe, not even ones with college degrees going around and punching lawmen."

He stepped closer to his boss. "They were torturing a lady. A young lady of your acquaintance. I had to stop them."

Paul Winslow reached into his jacket pocket and brought out a large wallet. "Katie? She's no lady. No, if this whole thing was over Katie, then that makes it even more tragic."

"She was a good worker for you. She did what she was told."

Paul Winslow thought about this. "True. That's one reason why I am going to miss that girl. She did what she was told to do. She wasn't no rebel like that Mags. I have put up with enough from that girl. Been getting the wrong ideas lately. I don't know who is to blame, but I want my obedient Negroes back. That's why I'm giving you all of your pay and telling you to get out of my town within twenty-four hours. If you don't, then I'll let my boys have you. And they are some kind of mad at you. Don't know what they'll do. You better not be around to find out." Paul Winslow held out some money.

Taking the money as his final pay, he said, "Your car is at the Bledsoe house."

"Yes, I'll get it from there," Paul Winslow said. Asa's face registered surprise as he continued. "You know, the boys were at the Bledsoe farm last night. I told them that since they couldn't find you, that they should pay the Bledsoes a visit. All cause of you. Those are some good people."

Asa struggled at this. "I hope that they didn't hurt anyone there. They didn't deserve that."

"Hmm. Hard to know what's happening when you are hiding out in the woods, isn't it?" He got back into the back of his car. "I want you gone today."

"No worries there, Mr. Winslow. I'll be sure to let your son know all about how well you are doing when I get back home."

Paul Winslow's eyes glazed over. "I have no son."

"Yes. Of course."

"Gone."

"I can't wait to see the backside of this backwater," Asa said to himself and folded the money into his pocket. Then, as fast as he could, he took up his cane and the few things he needed and moved quickly in the direction of the Bledsoe farm, hoping that it wasn't too late to help the Bledsoes or Mags.

If something happened to Mags, his most precious Pearl…

He could not afford to lose out a second time.

Chapter Sixteen

The scene in front of her was the stuff of Bledsoe nightmares. For years they had feared this happening, and it never had, until now.

Mags covered her own mouth for the fear of making too much noise and attracting their attention. She ducked back into the woods as she saw her family and the Carvers clustered together on the opposite end of the big wraparound porch.

What the nightriders had done was horrifying, but her family was safe. She took another path through the woods to the back of the farm and went toward the barn. She went up into the loft and crouched down low and she prayed.

Thank you God, thank you. Keep my family safe. Keep Asa safe. Keep everyone safe God please. She still did not come out because she didn't want to compromise her family's safety by letting them know where she was. There would be time enough for that in the morning. She laid on the small hayloft floor and, amidst the hay, she cried herself to sleep.

The squeak of the barn door woke her. It was her father as he came in to do his morning chores. "Daddy," she whispered. "I'm up here. Don't be scared."

"Oh praise Jesus," John Bledsoe cried. "Come on down from there, Margaret Ruth."

Mags alighted from the loft as quickly as she could and went into her father's arms. He embraced her tightly. She felt tears starting in her eyes again. How wonderful to know, before she left them potentially forever, that her family loved her, even as they weren't much for affection. "It's good to see you too, Daddy."

He held her out at arm's length and in the drawn skin on his neck, Mags could see evidence of the advancing years. What a difficult night this had been for him. "Your mama has been up all night, crying and praying for you."

"I've been out here most of the night, ever since the riders left. I didn't want to let you know I was out here in case they came back. You could honestly say that you didn't know where I was."

"Because that would lead to Asa. Always the sensible girl. I'm proud of you. Do you know where he is?"

"I took him to the old parsonage. I don't know where he is now." Despite herself, she got tears in her eyes again.

"You love him, don't you, girl?"

She could only nod, unable to move because she was so filled up with worry, concern, and love for Asa. "I'm happy to see that you found love, Mags, and that you finally realized that what you had with Travis was just a young thing. Puppy love."

"Yes, Daddy. I know that now. But I don't know where he is. He might be dead for all I know."

He put his arm around her. "Judging by the way he handled things last night, I would say he can handle himself. I feel at peace about it. I'm not worried about Asa and you shouldn't be either. Come on and help me with the chores so we can get you in to your mother."

"I'm going to get my things and say goodbye. It's best for me to go to Pittsburgh early. I'm going with him. It's not safe here for me anymore."

He put a hand on her elbow and patted her. "You're probably right. You need to go on up north to see your sister. I know that your mama will be upset that you won't be properly escorted, but you the daughter with the most sense. You'll be alright."

"Thank you, Daddy," Mags said with an air of sadness. It was hard, trying to slow down and not be efficient for once, knowing that this would be the last time in a long time that she could help her father with the chores.

When they were done, they took the milk pans into the kitchen in companionable silence, and Mags put them on the shelf. She used the kitchen sink to clean herself up as best as she could. When she was done and had put on a fresh apron, she turned and saw her mother watching her with tears in her eyes. They embraced tightly.

"I know that you have to do as you must, daughter. I'm proud of you. You don't know where Asa is?" Mags shook her head. Her mother continued, "Where ever he is, he is fine. Believe God will take care of him."

She nodded, trying not to cry. "I've started the biscuits, Mama."

"As I expected you would, once your daddy said you was here."

Basking in the glow of one last breakfast with her family, she tried to be cheery as she ate. Her sisters seemed especially long-faced and sad. It was better for her to go into her room and pack her bags. She had decided she would go into town and wait at Katie's family's house until the evening train came. Her father offered to take her into town, but Mags thought it was best that he did not come with her.

"Someone could grab you out there on the road, daughter." Brother Carver looked concerned.

"Then they would just get me, and not Daddy too," Mags said with more confidence than what she felt. Brother Carver was right. Would anyone want to grab her as she left? Did she matter than much?

"I can ride in the wagon up front and put you in the back and cover you as goods for the train," John said reasonably. "Like you say, I'll take you to Katie's family so that you can give them your condolences."

"I should go to the mill and get my back pay. He owes me money."

Lona looked afraid. "No, don't do that. Mr. Paul will know that he owes you and he will get it to us." Her mother turned to her father. "Tell her no, John." Lona's screaming made her father encircle his arms around her mother. "She be walking right into the devil's parlor."

"I make sure she get to the train, Lona. Calm down now."

Mags left the kitchen where her parents were carrying on and went to the car. She felt around inside where Asa told her to go and she found the notebook.

When she drew it out, it was almost warm as if it were a live pulsating thing. To some extent it was. She took it and put it into a pocket in her skirt. She wanted to keep it close to her body.

The notebook felt like protection for her and so many others. The words it held were the reason was why Asa was risking his life. The mules were hitched to the wagon. Her sisters stood in a little clutch together on the porch, crying.

"These is terrible times," Em said.

"They are, my little pretties," Mags said to them. "I'll be back."

"No," Nettie said. "You're going to marry Asa and leave us behind in old Winslow."

She lifted her arms to embrace her sisters squeezing tight. She focused on Nettie, the sister closest in age to her. Did Nettie know something she didn't? Everyone had always joked about Nettie's "knowing things." She was the most pious one of them. She had God's ear, and he heard her prayers.

"Net." She grasped her sister's hands. "I don't even know if Asa is alive. They might have found him in the parsonage and lynched him. I'm going up there, not even knowing if he will come."

"Sister. Have faith in the Lord. He'll see you through. His goodness shines like a light in all of this. He knows what is right and what is not right. It's right and good that Asa be your husband. And when he is, try not to boss him too much like you boss us." Nettie smiled at her and they embraced.

"I love you all," Mags told them as she got into the back of the wagon. Despite the hot July morning, her father covered her up with quilts and blankets.

Bracing herself, she laid down and tried not to look up at all. She had to trust what was coming and not question the road ahead.

The sun rose up, and he was not exactly sure where he was going, but he just kept walking, relying on faith to let him know he was headed in the right direction. Sweat poured down him in the July morning. He had walked so far on his leg, farther than he had ever done, and he would have to stop and rest. The distance had seemed much shorter when he took it with Mags last night. Was being with her that made the journey less arduous and more bearable?

Please, God, help me find my way. Please stay by my side.

He followed the small creek stream, knowing it would lead him to the Bledsoe farm eventually. Occasionally he would stop, have a drink and soothe the ache in his stump leg. Would it take him the twenty-four hours he had been given to get out of this terribly forsaken place?

He remembered how much pride his mother took in letting people know that the Masons, her people, had been in Pittsburgh since the Civil War. As OPs, Old Pittsburghers, they were not recent transplants to Pittsburgh people she felt were overrunning the city. They had been there already, and certainly had not been foolish enough to stay in the South where Negroes had continued to be treated poorly.

However, making his way, step by step through the thick woods, he knew that these people were no fools. They were survivors and brave and deserved better than the persecution they got in wanting better lives for their children.

He thought of his slave ancestors, and instead of the shame that he usually felt about having had them, he understood the strength it took for them to survive. And because they had survived, he was determined to as well. With his survival, he was compelled to pass the story on to his own children and family. Children. With Mags.

He couldn't help but smile to himself when he thought of Mags. However, when he thought of introducing her to his mother, his smile disappeared. He did not care. Elodie Mason Caldwell would just have to deal with his choice of a wife, and he didn't care anymore in choosing someone who she would approve of just because of skin color. If he were being honest with himself, and there was no better time than now to be honest, that was the appeal in his relationship with Aline. His mother would have approved of her whiteness. Now he could see just how wrong that all was. Aline was dead and part of him still missed her, but his marriage to her would have been an unjust use of her.

He thought again of Mags standing firm over him and his heart warmed. He had to make his way to her. He could see better light through the trees and he cautiously broke through, trying to see where he was. Foolishly, he had gone further than what he needed and he was on a road between the Bledsoe farm and the Winslow spread. Now, there was no more cover of woods between here and the farm, so he would just have to make way to the Bledsoes in the open space. Now he cared. Because he wanted a life with Mags.

Please, do not let me be discovered. Please. Hide me.

He had almost made it to the open back area where the Bledsoe barn was when he heard the clip clop of hooves. His heart raced and his palms felt clammy, but he had to turn around to meet his destiny. John Bledsoe. Their eyes met at the exact same time and John gave a cry of surprise.

"I know that you almost to the yard, but get in the back. I take you on to the house. I just dropped Margaret off in town."

His heart swelled to hear it. "How is she?"

"She's fine. She getting ready to take the Express in the morning. How about you?"

Asa breathed out. "I'll be more than ready. Take me to her."

John shook his head. "No offense, but you look a mess. Best go on back into the house and Lona will get you straightened out. I got to take Brother and Sister in on the same train and it'll be a few hours. You need a hot meal. You can't go to my daughter just looking like anything. "

"No, sir, I can't." Asa got into the back of the wagon and rested, glad to be discovered by the right person at last.

After a proper farewell, her father had dropped her off into the yard of Katie's house. Katie's mother had come out onto the porch to wrap her arms around her, weeping. "I had been wondering where she get all that fancy stuff. I just can't believe that she would go and be with Mr. Paul like that. I raise her better than that. Mags, I loved my girl, but knowing this now, what I didn't know before? It's mighty hard."

"I know, ma'am." She knew how to comfort. She got to work, boiling a tea drink and forced it on Mrs. Marshall, trying to calm her down.

"And now you are going too? Ain't no one going to be left in Winslow no more."

"I'm going to help Ruby, ma'am, and then I'll be back."

Katie's mother shook her head. "No. No. You won't be back. You see how much better the treatment is up there. I got a brother, he live in Cleveland and he telling me all the time to leave here. Now that my girl is gone, I just might do that. I'm sorry that you can't stay for the funeral."

"I'm sorry too," Mags said. "I would have liked to say goodbye to Katie. I'm sorry."

Katie's mother wiped her wet face with a handkerchief. "What you got to apologize about child?"

"If I had stood up sooner to stop her, I might have led her away and avoided all of that trouble. But I was angry at her and I didn't help as soon as I could."

Crumbling up a handkerchief, Mrs. Marshall looked her square in the face. "Listen. Everything that Katie did, she decided to do. She decided to lay down with that dog, Mr. Paul. She decided to tell him everything you was doing. She made up her mind to get all them little trinkets and things from him in exchange for what she does. She the one who was in a shameful way. That all her, not you. Not a thing you can do about it. Let go, child. Go on and live your life."

When some other women friends came and started visiting with Katie's mother, she took it as an opportunity to let them know she was going into town to get her money for the trip together. Katie's mother looked concerned, but she was so full of her own grief, she said nothing to Mags.

So, she decided to take her walk to the mill, knowing how her mother would not have been pleased by her decision. Still, Paul Winslow was going to pay for her trip.

When she got to the mill, things looked in disarray. That's not how she would have had it, but still, she knocked on Paul Winslow's office door, an unusual thing for her. Usually, she would have left him a note requesting a chance to meet with him, or asked someone else to let him know.

He didn't answer. She knew he had to be here, so she sat down to wait.

After about fifteen minutes of waiting, Paul Winslow came to his office door and saw her dressed in her second best and not in her mill clothes. His appearance was rumpled, but he was not the least bit disturbed to see her. "You late, Mags? It ain't no matter. I fired that uppity Negro and told him to get his black butt out of my town. You need to get back on the floor and start your being in charge again. You back on to five dollars a day as of now, but I'm going to have to dock your pay for these hours that you missed this morning."

"I want to talk to you." She started to shake, but stilled herself, trying to remain calm about what she had heard. Was Asa still alive? Is that what he meant?

"What, girl?" He acted as if she were a fly, a little nothing that was bothering him. "You got your job back. Go on and get on your machine."

She stepped closer to him and this forced him into his office. "I said, I wanted to talk to you."

"Margaret, what is wrong with you? Get in here."

She knew that he was really shaken because he called her Margaret instead of girl. She followed him into his office and closed the door against the noise of the mill. "I'm going up to Pittsburgh today. I need money for my train ticket."

"What? Train tickets cost plenty of money, girl, I might not have it. What are you talking about?"

"Fifteen dollars."

Paul Winslow whistled. "I don't know if I got all of that. Sounds to me like if you don't have the money, you better stay here at home."

"I'm supposed to go up North and help Ruby with her baby."

"Oh, I'm sure that Dr. Morson has that all taken care of. They don't need you. You aren't a nurse. You're a mill hand. There ain't no helping with a baby when you are a mill hand."

Mags cleared her throat. "I'm not sure you understand, sir. I'm quitting. I want my money so I can leave."

Paul Winslow sat up. "You can't quit on me, girl."

"Yes, I'm doing that, sir. Yesterday was my last day."

"I don't owe you anywhere near no fifteen dollars. If that is what you need to leave, then you can't go."

"I know that you don't owe me that in my pay. You owe me $3.25. But I feel that you know that you should give me the fifteen dollars that I'm asking you for."

"Why should I do that?"

"Ruby. Adam. Solomon. The new baby. Katie. And you owe it to me. I've made you richer over this past year than you ever have been. So, I feel that you'll give it to me, sir, because you know you owe it to me."

"I ought to fire you for speaking to me like this."

"I'm quitting, sir. You cannot fire me."

Paul Winslow fixed her with a strong stare. She stared back at him. She would not back down. He reached for his wallet and a small thrill of victory traced through her. He laid a twenty-dollar bill on his desk. "Go on and take it. I don't have any change."

Picking up the money with shaking fingers, she marveled at the strange currency. She had never seen so much money at once before in her life. "Thank you."

"When is this baby due? You best be back after it is born."

"The baby is due in August."

"Yeah. Okay. August. You better be back before the end of August or you'll lose your job. Permanently."

"Yes, sir," she said. There was no use in contradicting what he said. She had gotten what she wanted.

"You'll be interested to know that I left that uppity Negro out there in the woods. I won't ever be hiring someone like that again. I prefer old home folk."

Her heart skipped a few beats. How had he left him? "What was he doing when you left him, sir?"

Paul Winslow laughed. "He probably trying to figure out how to get out of the woods. Couldn't go far on that leg of his anyhow."

Something in her died while Paul Winslow laughed and taunted a man who had fought for his country and all he had to show for it was a Bakelite leg.

Thank the dear Lord she had not enacted her plans of revenge against him. The words were right. Let God handle Paul Winslow and his unspeakable cruelties.

What had happened to Asa, though, and how would he meet up with her? Nettie's words haunted the edge of her thoughts. Trust in God to help them find the way to help them be together.

Chapter Seventeen

All day long, Mags felt a pressure on her legs with Asa's notebook and the money in her pocket. Still, she felt a triumph whenever she thought about her confrontation with Paul Winslow and understood how David must have felt when he triumphed over Goliath.

When she returned to Katie's mother's house, she used her organizing skills to help the woman handle the onslaught of visitors who were coming to convey their condolences at Katie's death. It wasn't all of the visitation that she would receive today, she knew, still, the numbers represented a measure of the generosity of the people of Winslow. She really wished that she could stay and help further, but her train left that night at 8:03 p.m. and she knew that she should be on it.

The mill housing wasn't far from the train station and when it was time, at about 7:30 p.m., she said goodbye to Katie's family and began the ten-minute walk to the train station. She ignored the suspicious looks that the trainmaster gave her when she presented her twenty-dollar bill to pay for her ticket, but she didn't care. The first train would take her to Atlanta, and she would transfer to The Crescent Express, which would take her all the way through Philadelphia where she would have to change to a train going westward to get to Pittsburgh. She wished that she could send a telegram to Ruby and Adam telling them that she was coming early, but maybe there would be time when she reached Philadelphia. No doubt, this was a fearful thing, going alone, but she would do what she had to do. And pray for Asa to join her. She sat down on the platform to wait when, coming around the corner, were the Carvers.

"What are you all doing here? You should be at the revival." She stood to greet them and they hugged her.

"Child, we felt it better to go on ahead to our son. We gave a brief prayer at the revival and then turned it on over to Nettie to do," Brother Carver said.

Nettie—doing the revival meeting? Her mind reeled. She wished she could be there to see it. "We going to get on out of here. There's so much hatred going around now." Sister Jane threw her hands up as she saw Brother Carver step over to the trainmaster to exchange their tickets.

Her father stepped up onto the platform and she ran to him and hugged him another time. "Daddy, it is so good to see you. They said Net is doing the meeting?"

"She is." John beamed. "She was wonderful, at least the part that I saw. She bringing some real healing to these folks who are hurting because of Katie." The look on his face became stormy. "There weren't no police there either. I think they thought people would be afraid to gather."

"The attendance was low," Brother Carver admitted. "But I think that's because people didn't know that Net was going to do the meeting."

She smiled. "That's wonderful." She looked puzzled as Brother Carver handed her a ticket. "No, I have a ticket."

"What? Did you go over to that mill?"

"I did. He gave me the money."

John shook his head. "Your mama won't be happy. Guess this ticket will have to be turned in for another passenger."

Her father went back out and gestured around the corner. She followed her father and saw Asa come out from the back of the wagon, carrying his grip. She ran down the stairs to him and they embraced. "I made it," he said.

"I'm so glad that you did." The feeling was so full in her, she wanted to cry, but she couldn't.

"I want to do as I promised. I told Ruby I was going to bring you and I am."

"I was worried about how to let them know I was coming."

"We may have time to send notice once we reach Philadelphia." Asa kept a tight arm around her waist and she felt secure in his hold.

"Come on up to the platform now," John called. "You all don't want to miss the train."

She watched as Asa adjusted himself and used his cane to climb up the stairs to the platform, carrying his grip by himself. She could see that he was winded when he got to the top of the stairs, but he made it. They could hear the train whistle in the distance. She gave her father one last hug and Asa shook his hand.

"We be seeing them to Atlanta, John. We change trains for Florida there," Brother Carver informed them.

"Send word for safety as soon as you can," John Bledsoe's voice came thick.

"You go on now, Daddy. Take care. You need to get home before dark yourself," she said, urging her father on.

"I'll take good care of her, sir," Asa said.

"I have no doubt that you will." John smiled and they watched him as he got behind the mules and drove off. Her heart nearly leaped into her throat as she saw the train coming down the track.

But, was that Paul Winslow and the lawmen approaching them from the other side of the platform? It was and he came and stood in front of them.

"What are you doing here?" she shouted over the coming train.

"My boys want to make an arrest here. They are trying to see if they can."

"This is ridiculous," Asa said, linking his arm through hers. "You told me to get out of your town within twenty-four hours and I'm doing it. What do you want?"

"I want you out, but your lady, she needs to stay here with me."

Brother Carver started praying out loud.

Sister glared at Paul Winslow. "We're all leaving. The way you treats these people in this town is just shameful. I don't know if we are coming back for any more revivals. It's so terrible folks can't come and go as they want."

"This here is none of your affair," Paul Winslow said smoothly. He grabbed

Mags by her elbow and she startled. He had never, ever, touched her.

Asa stood right in front of his handhold. "I'm telling you kindly, sir," he shouted as the train pulled up to them. "Let her go."

She tried to wrestle herself from his grip, but his hold on her was like iron. "She ain't going nowhere with you. You get on that train."

The lawmen stepped forward and brandished their weapons.

"Jesus." Sister Jane stepped forward. "Turn her loose, now, please."

She stared up at the urgency in Sister Jane's voice, but what made her really fearful was the strange look in Paul Winslow's eyes. His eyes had no emotion, or feeling in them. They were just cold. Empty.

"Asa, please get on the train."

"I'm not leaving you."

Inside her mind, she searched for an answer. "Mr. Paul," she said in the old time speak, "Miss Mary would be ashamed at this. I told you I'll never leave Winslow. Not really. Please, let me get on the train and go to Ruby to help her. I got a feeling she going to have a girl and if she does, I'll tell her to name her Mary, because of you being so kind."

Then, the sorrow came back in his eyes, and she knew he thought of his dead wife. That slip of emotion, just that little bit of caring, made his grip less than strong and she eased out of his hold. "Let's go," she said to Asa and they all climbed up, taking time to see that Asa got on. They had to board on Jim Crow cars, at least until they got into Pennsylvania, which had rough wooden benches. She had heard and read a lot about Jim Crow cars, but being able to leave made it look like a paradise to her.

They sat down on one spare bench and Asa put her inside by the window, so that she could hear Paul Winslow still yelling after her. "You best be back. I know you for a good Christian girl. You wouldn't lie, now."

"And we know you for the very devil," Asa muttered under his breath in her ear. "You'll never come back here. Ever."

She gave a quick prayer of gratitude that she was on the train, despite the conditions. When she lifted her eyes, she saw the desperate looking face of Paul

Winslow who had kept her in his sights following the train little bit by little bit.

And she knew God had his vengeance.

That man didn't know it, but his entire world had changed. The powerful Paul Winslow looked small and desperate. Something in her heart felt sad at this pitiful display. The great Paul Winslow was following a Jim Crow car down the train platform.

"I'll tell you one thing." She slipped her hand into the crook of Asa's arm. "I bet he has never been to a train to see any Negroes off. Times sure have changed." She laid her head on his shoulder and breathed out, reveling in each breath. This time spent with Asa was indeed a gift from God to be very thankful for.

Traveling Jim Crow was hard, and the wooden benches were a reminder that they had no soft places in their existence. Also, not having access to the same accommodations as others did made him want to punch things. Still, everything was made easier by being accompanied by Mags, who never having been on a train before, and saw everything from new eyes and perspectives.

When they left Brother Carver and Sister Jane in Atlanta, her last touch of home, they spread out because the Jim Crow car emptied out. She laid down on one of the hard, wooden benches and went to sleep. He stayed up all night and watched her. In some ways, she seemed so young and naïve at twenty years old. Did she really understand what she was getting into with him? Still, his Pearl deserved credit. She had shown such poise and strength of character over these past few days when there had been a lot of trouble. He was proud of her and so proud to be with her. He hadn't realized that he had gone to sleep because when he woke up, he saw that she was looking at him.

"Philadelphia's still a few hours away and I'm hungry."

"Your mama gave me lunch."

"Miss Katie's mother let me make one up out of all of the food that came to the house, so I guess we are both well prepared."

The two of them came to the conclusion that they liked Lona's chicken the best. There was a piece of pound cake, though, in her lunch that was pretty good, and they both came to the consensus that it would be hard to come across some pound cake like that, even though Mags did a pretty good job when she made it.

The recollections made her sad, so he tried to distract her. "When we get off of the train, just stay with me. I'll make sure that we get word to Pittsburgh somehow to have someone meet us. We can eat another lunch in Philadelphia if we want."

"I won't know where I'm going. It sounds pretty good to me."

When they disembarked from the train, he could see Mags was pretty overwhelmed by the largeness of the Philadelphia train station. He went to a desk and sent a telegram message to his mother and to Adam Morson saying they were coming in. He certainly hoped that Adam would meet them, even as he knew it was a risk since the doctor could be busy.

After they had lunch in a restaurant where the diners were not separated by race, they got on the train where there were plush velvet seats for them to sit on. If all went well, they would be in Pittsburgh in time for a late supper. He could see that she was pretty wowed by everything, even by the conductor taking her ticket and calling her "Miss."

"He called me Miss. A white man." Mags shook her head after the conductor had walked away from them.

"That's how it is up here. Some of the time."

"It's amazing. You get used to being treated a certain way for so long, that when someone is nice to you, it's shocking. It shouldn't be like that."

"No. You deserve nice treatment all of the time."

Mags patted her hair. "I hope I can freshen up a little more before I get to Pittsburgh. I wouldn't want them to see me looking country."

"You look lovely." He meant every word of it. He only hoped his mother would be able to understand how he felt from his point of view. It didn't matter and he didn't care what she said. Mags was his.

He could see that she was entranced by the Pennsylvania countryside of his birth. Mags sounded as if she had learned something from her schooling when she said, "It's still part of the Appalachian mountain range, so it's hilly. But it's all brown and green instead of red and green."

He smiled at her comment. "Yes that's true."

"How does the brown come out of clothes?" Mags wondered.

"I think that people from up here wonder the same thing about your Georgia red clay."

"Will there be church tomorrow?"

"Oh yes. There is always church. We belong to one of the biggest and most prominent Negro congregations in Pittsburgh. My mother and your sister run just about everything in the church."

"I just can't believe it. Ruby was never one for church leadership—she always made fun of mama, who is the one at First Water in charge of things. You saw."

"I did. You'll have to see for yourself tomorrow."

When they got closer to Pittsburgh, the air got thicker and foggier looking. Mags was disappointed that she couldn't get a better view of the city as they came closer. "It's the industry," he said. "The steel mills. They fire all of the time, day and night and make the air like that. I've been in the clear, clean, country air for so long, I forgot about this. Still, it's better where we are in the Hill District because we are up on a hill. The train station is down in a valley, I suppose and that's why the air is thick."

When the train stopped, he gathered their luggage up and steered her out to the front where all of the hansom cabs were lined up. He craned his neck and saw that across the street from the train station, there was a single gray hansom cab with an elegant initial on the side—the old intertwined "EM." His mother sure knew how to travel in style. "She's across the street," he gestured and dear Mags patted her hair again as if she were nervous, following him carefully.

Elodie Mason Caldwell was sitting in the back of a double-seated hansom cab and held her arms out to her son. He fell into them with a warm embrace in return. "Mother, it's good to see you. Thank you so much for coming to get me."

"You had to have the proper ride back to be able to rest your leg. You look different. Who is this?" His mother drew back in surprise.

"I told you that we were coming together. This is Ruby's sister, Margaret."

"Ruby? Ruby Morson?"

"That's right. She's come to help her with the baby and the house."

"Her sister?" Elodie Caldwell looked as if she had lost all of her senses in her confusion. "But she looks nothing like her."

Shrinking up and sliding away in between the Pittsburgh cobblestones seemed like the best alternative to having to hear his mother's words. He knew precisely what his mother meant, although he wasn't sure that Mags did. He needn't have worried. She stepped forward and offered her hand.

He quailed a bit. While he loved holding Mags's hands, they weren't the hands of a lady. Her hands were the hands of a worker and she was not wearing gloves. He doubted that Elodie had shaken the hands of a worker often. "I look like my father, Mrs. Caldwell and Ruby favors our mother. So good to finally meet you."

"Yes." The limp handshake that his mother offered was not very welcoming. "Welcome to Pittsburgh."

He handed her into the carriage. Mags sat on the opposite side from Elodie and moved over to make room for Asa. "Oh no, dear. It's better for him over here, there's his leg you see."

He got into the carriage and sat next to his mother, where his leg was cramped, but he knew that Elodie was asserting her authority as she always did. He didn't want to say anything just now, but he would soon. His mother put her hand on his arm and leaned in. "Your telegram didn't come in time to alert your sisters, but they'll be at church tomorrow and will see you then. Oh son, it is so good that you are home and away from that dreadful place. It just isn't safe for a son of a prominent family to travel down there anymore. Promise me that you won't."

"I'm going to be in Pittsburgh a bit to do some writing, so I'm not looking to go anywhere anytime soon." He tried to make eye contact with Mags, but she wouldn't look at him. She seemed sad somehow, deflated, and he wanted to let her know that everything was alright.

"We can drop her off, um. What's your name again, dear?"

"Margaret, ma'am."

"Oh yes. We can drop her off at the Morsons' before we go home. It seems as if the month that you have been gone was so long and we heard so little from you."

"It would be dangerous to send mail, Mama. It's hard to know who is reading the mails that go in and out."

"That's terrible. Imagine a place like that where you can't even send a letter. Dreadful."

"Well, I had to go down there to investigate and to bring Pearl back here to her sister."

"Pearl? Who calls her that?"

"I do," Asa asserted.

His mother laughed. "She's about as far from a pearl as you can get. Asa, I swear, the things that you say."

"She had a dreadful name down there. Mags." He seemed to have to reach a long way to clasp her hand and it was awkward. "I changed it. Now that she's here, she'll be Pearl."

"Oh for heaven's sake. Margaret is a perfectly suitable name. That's what I will call her."

"Then Pearl will be my special name for her." He squeezed Mags's hand a bit before he let go.

All signs of smiles disappeared from Elodie Caldwell. "You came up here unescorted, then? Have you been married before, Margaret?"

"No, ma'am." Her answer, although respectful, was loaded with emotion.

"Well, that's something isn't it? Who would think to travel all of that way without an escort? I guess things are different in the South."

"We had an escort as far as Atlanta." He let his mother know.

Mags spoke up. "We could not arrange for another one when we left, since our lives were at stake. There are times when propriety cannot be followed."

Thankfully, the carriage was coming closer to Ruby's house and he breathed a sigh of relief. "We cared, Mama. The war has changed things, you know? I didn't lay a hand on her." He winked at Mags, who gave him a straightforward look. "And she didn't lay a hand on me."

"I would certainly hope not," Elodie said, clearly shocked at the very idea.

The carriage slowed down and stopped in front of Ruby's brownstone in the Lower Hill. His mother's house was higher and a few streets over from Ruby's house. "Here's where Ruby and Adam live." He got out of the carriage and helped Mags out. He reached in the back, going for her bag, but Elodie interrupted.

"Let Simon get that. I didn't raise you to be a stevedore. Get back into the carriage Asa, we're late for supper."

Asa took Mags to the door and knocked on it, resolving to pay his mother no mind, knocking on the door. "Well, here you are."

"Yes, here I am." Mags informed him in a flat voice. "Thank you for seeing me here."

"I'll see you at church in the morning and then you will come to mother's house for lunch."

"Must I?"

"She's my mother."

Mags looked Elodie over as she sat there in the carriage and she looked him up and down. "Funny. You don't look like her at all. Or maybe you just act like her."

A servant opened the door and he told her who Mags was. Ruby and Adam were famous for their revolving doors of help and he was somewhat surprised to see Ruby had held on to the same servant who had been there last month. Maybe someone was catching on to Ruby's ways. Still, it warmed him as he retreated to hear a loud shriek of delight as the Bledsoe sisters reunited and Mags got the warm welcome she deserved.

It was hard though, to erase the look of disappointment on Mags's face from his mind. When he got back to the carriage, he sat on the opposite side where Mags had been, facing his mother.

"Goodness, it's something when these country ones come in. If you had not told me she was Ruby's sister, I would have never, ever believed it. She's so dark."

"So what? She's beautiful, Mother."

"Yes, of course, Asa. She's very attractive and dignified for a country person, I'll give her that, even though, as I said, I question her judgment in traveling with you all of that way unescorted."

"She was nearly stopped from getting on the train in the first place, just because she was so important to the economy down there. The whites are not happy at the number of Negroes coming north."

"Indeed?" Elodie's face made a puzzle. "Well, it's a good thing that she won't be here long, isn't it? There's too many of those country people up here as it is."

He opened his mouth to correct her, but he gave up. Elodie would know soon enough and she would just have to get used to Mags as her daughter-in-law.

He needed to make sure he had his own place all ready for Mags, so that he could provide for her. She shouldn't have to be in his mother's house, where Mags would probably run the place better than she did. One woman in that house was more than enough.

Chapter Eighteen

When Mags went into Ruby's house, she resolved to put everything, and she meant everything that was on the other side of the door behind her and enjoy her sister's house.

First of all, Ruby had a servant, a very young girl that was probably about Nettie's age, and probably newly arrived from the south herself, given her soft accent. Next, when she walked in, she was astonished at the large open quality of the rooms, and how well appointed they were with heavy oak furniture. The girl led her down a long hallway and Mags could see up a tall staircase where the bedrooms where.

"The doctor, he sees people in the back way, so's folks can come in without disturbing the family. He got someone back there now."

"I need to see..." Mags gulped, "...Mrs. Morson."

"She stay up in her room most of the time. She supposed to. Doctor tell her to."

"Get up here, Mags!" Ruby yelled down the stairs and tears started at the corners of her eyes at the sound of her sister's voice, a voice she had not heard for four long years.

"But she doesn't stay does she?" She took off her hat, placing her grip in the hallway.

"Naw, ma'am." The girl shook her head sadly.

"I'm sure that you have other duties. I'll go and see her myself."

"Yes, ma'am." The girl looked at her, seemingly shocked at Mags's confidence. Clearly she had far more nerve than the girl did, and she was only newly arrived in Pittsburgh.

The feeling of the wooden banister under her hand as she climbed the staircase almost made the hurt in her heart go away. Almost. Standing on the landing before the second set of stairs, she could see through the distorted window glass the retreating back of the hansom cab and the back of Asa's well-shaped head.

That is the end of that. Mags climbed the next landing of stairs, astonished at how well her sister and her husband were doing in this beautiful brownstone. When she got to the top of the stairs, rooms stretched in either direction with the floors carpeted in fancy patterned rugs, and the hallway lined up with potted greenery plants, almost like bushes.

In one of the rooms to the right, a sweet voice piped up brought some balm to her aching heart. "I don't want to go to bed, Mama."

Ruby's soprano trilled in reply. "Solomon, you go to bed or there will be no pudding. Do what mama says."

Mags started walking in the same direction as the voice and before she knew it, she appeared in a doorway where her sister lay in a huge four-poster bed. Her little nephew came to her legs like a shooting star, and Mags braced them in time to catch him in her arms and inhaled the sweet small child scent of him.

Solomon was a beautiful child, with long silky black locks and a beautiful little white frock that was clearly dirty with jam, and who knew what else. "Let's go to your mama. We'll make her feel better by doing as she asks." Amazingly, Solomon took up her hand without any questions as if he knew her.

"Oh, Mags. I prayed about it, but I never thought you would come." Ruby put her hands over her face and began to sob. *Just like Mama would.* And Ruby had said she would never be like their mother.

Mags and Solomon scrambled up on the bed next to Ruby and Mags embraced her sister as best as she could. When she withdrew from Ruby, their faces were both wet with sweat and tears, not knowing or caring which was which. She reached down and kissed Ruby on the forehead, the only vacant space where she could. Looking at her sister's face, Mags noted the dark circles under her eyes and didn't like the look of it. A sharp pang of worry invaded her heart. She wasn't a medical person, but Ruby's belly seemed so stretched and distended under the bed covers that she touched the hard roundness there. "I'm here, sister. Early, but I am here."

"I give thanks to God. There are terrible, terrible things happening all over and I didn't want you to get caught up in any of it."

"I didn't."

"I knew you would make it with Asa Caldwell escorting you."

Her heard jumped a bit at the sound of his real name. "I'm fine. I made it here. And just in time to help you apparently." She grabbed at Solomon's little arm. "Who is this filthy young man?"

"I'm Solomon, Auntie. And I don't want a bath."

"You need one. I'm going to take you down to the kitchen and scrub you good."

Ruby smiled at her. "We have indoor plumbing. The bathroom is down the hall."

"The bathroom?" Mags pulled back in disbelief. "They have rooms for that in fairy stories."

"We got one here." Ruby spread her hands and rested them on her belly.

"Amazing."

"It's just me who isn't holding up my end of the bargain."

Mags patted her sister's hand. "Stop that now. I know that he loves you more than ever."

"He does. I just feel guilty about it, that's all. So I try to do what I can from here, but it's all a hopeless mess."

"And I suspect that little girl downstairs doesn't do much, does she?"

Ruby shook her head. "I've needed you so, Mags."

"I can see that, Mrs. Doctor, and I'm going to help you starting now with this filthy one."

"Do I hafta listen to her?" Solomon fixed his big black eyes on her with mistrust.

"Yes. I'm your Auntie Mags, and you must do what I say."

"Great. More grownups telling me what to do." Solomon put his chin in his hands. He looked so cute, she had to bite her lip to keep from laughing.

"You need it you bad thing, you. Mama is at her wits end with you, spoiled thing." Ruby leaned back, throwing up her hands.

"Don't worry, Ruby. I'll make sure that he is clean, and if he is good, he can have a pudding and a story about what a trouble maker he was as a baby." Mags stood and held her hand out to Solomon. To her surprise, he took it and meekly followed.

"I'll have a rest, Mags. Then, come back to me and tell me all, please do. I've been longing for home so much."

"Of course," Mags promised her sister and let Solomon lead her to the wonder that was a bathroom in her sister's home. She was glad, for Ruby's sake, that Adam was doing so well in his practice.

What a blessing to be needed somewhere. It made things easier. Since she was needed here, she could forget all about Asa Caldwell. And his mother.

The firm pressure and feel of his moustache on her mouth haunted her and made her tingle.

It would not be easy.

The congregation of Freedom Christian was large as Asa said. For the past two years, it had been the mission of its leading church ladies, Ruby and Elodie, to help the stream of southern transplants to find work and places to live when they arrived in Pittsburgh.

Grateful for the outreach provided, the new arrivals came to Pittsburgh and learned the ways of the urban city and they began to prosper, the numbers of the church swelled. The ministers were grateful to these powerful ladies for the ways they provided the outreach, but when Ruby had been repeatedly with child, a lot of the workload fell by the wayside.

The opportunity was perfect for Mags's organizing capacities and he couldn't wait to tell her so. He had never been so eager to escort his mother to church, knowing he was going to see his Pearl. In the light of day, he would make sure that his mother had a better understanding of who she was to him and how important she was.

When he arrived and looked over at the Morson pew where he expected to see the family, a sharp pang was in his heart at the emptiness. It consumed his thoughts all service long. He almost did not hear when Reverend Fairgate cited him in the church membership as someone who was doing great works for the Negro population. Consumed with thoughts of Mags's beautiful swan-like neck and the gracious tilt of her head, he rubbed his hands together in hope.

How would Mags meet his sisters if she didn't come to Sunday lunch? Sunday lunch was always a large buffet type affair in his mother's ornate parlor. The buffet usually consisted of cold meats, vegetables and desserts. He didn't want to go, though, if it meant that Mags would not be there to meet his family. When he escorted his mother out to the carriage, he mentioned the missing Morsons.

"I hope all is okay with Sister Ruby. I expected to see them at church."

His mother gave him a sharp look. "She's had a difficult time. Her husband has confined her to bed and he's not able to keep a close eye on her with his practice. Solomon cannot come by himself. They have had a revolving staff of people come and go. I've tried to help them, but I have my own place to run and my own things to take care of."

"Maybe I should go see them and extend my greetings. I'm not done yet writing my report, but I can share some of my initial findings with them."

"Everyone, and I do mean everyone, will be expecting you at luncheon. You cannot go over to the Morsons', uninvited."

"I would not be uninvited," Asa said knowing that "dropping in" would be a terrible breach of etiquette. He was inclined to forget all about the proper way of things. He had to know if Mags was angry at him.

"Regardless, you must be at luncheon. That's all."

Asa was glad to see his sisters, as well as his nieces and nephews as they all came to luncheon, hurriedly shoving cold-roasted chicken and slices of beef down their throats. Still, it struck him that there was something dry about his mother's food and it stuck in his throat. He would never admit it to Elodie, but Mags was a better cook. What would Sunday lunch be if Mags were hostessing? Maybe less formal, more comfortable? What would it be like for her to preside over her own space, rather than adjust to some other woman's kitchen? He intended to make the invitation to her by way of a marriage proposal just as soon as he could get away.

His mother went upstairs to lie down and his sisters remained behind to catch up and to get his nieces and nephews in gear. That was his opportunity for escape from the suffocating parlor. He went out back, saddled one of the horses, and used the riding block to ease himself onto the horse's back. As quickly he could, he made his way to Ruby and Adam's house, thinking of an excuse he could use to see Mags.

When Ruby suggested that she stay home with them for church, Mags was rather relieved. She didn't want to say so to her sister, but if Elodie was in charge of things in the church, she didn't want to run into that snobbishness so soon. Mags woke on that Sunday morning, and she made a breakfast of porridge. She, Solomon and Ruby laid up on the bed and listened as Adam read scripture from a chair next to the bed.

She requested that her brother-in-law read Corinthians, chapter thirteen, which had some special resonance for her today. "When I was a child, I spake as a child, but when I became a man I put away childish things." It had been a favorite verse of their Uncle Arlo's. When Adam asked for prayer, Mags bowed her head and wiped away at her face. She said an extra special prayer for the baby, feeling very selfish, and stood up right away to clean the kitchen and develop a list in her mind for the maid, Elsie. She would direct her in her new duties now that she had arrived. No, she had never had a maid before, but she had had sisters. She tied a head scarf on her bounteous hair and went to work.

Even on a Sunday, Adam had patients to see and she reassured him she would help in the house so that he could be in his office, doing his work. Adam offered to take Solomon to the park after lunch and Mags was grateful. Solomon was a lovely child, but he had a great deal of energy that needed to be diverted. She resolved to ask Adam what, if anything, could be done for the inquisitive boy and his education. He would do well to learn his letters.

When Adam and Solomon left, Ruby rested in the quiet house and Mags did not want to disturb her. After giving Elsie direction, she felt in need of a rest herself. She had let the maid have off Sunday afternoon so Mags resolved to go into the parlor and put her feet up.

How special to have a parlor where Ruby could rest any time that she wanted to. It made Ruby's success that much more apparent. Putting her feet up on an overstuffed ottoman she instantly laid her head back and drifted off. She had spent much of the night crying and feeling sorry for herself.

Her house didn't even have to be this fancy, but she wanted one. Maybe, once they did go to the church, she would find her own husband at Freedom. The front door knocker sounded and she jolted awake, heading for the door, determined not to let the sound wake her resting sister. Maybe it was a patient or Adam and Solomon coming back from the park. But it wouldn't make sense for them to knock on their own front door, knowing that Ruby was confined to her bed. And the patients came to a special entrance at the back of the house.

She went to the front door and lifted the latch. Asa stood before her. "Well, just who I was hoping to see," he said. His voice sounded a bit loud.

"Hello, Mr. Thomas. May I help you with something?"

"Well, Mags, you don't have to sound like that about it. I've come to see you."

"Were you invited?"

"Ruby and Adam are my friends." he said, nonplussed at her question.

"Ruby is resting and Adam took Solomon to the park." Mags began to push the heavy wooden door shut. "I'm here, in effect, by myself and it wouldn't be decent to let you in. I cannot allow you inside, nor can you see me in the presence of my sister because she is confined to her bedroom. So, as you can see, your visit is very inconvenient just now."

"I just wanted to apologize for the way my mother acted yesterday."

"If she wanted to apologize for how she had acted, she could do it for herself. Is she here?" Mags made a show of looking around. "I didn't think so." She pushed on the door to close it up.

Asa put a hand on the door to stop her. "I thought you would be at church today where she could speak to you and you could meet my family and come over for luncheon."

"We must have a care for Ruby's health. These days, the family doesn't go out much and I cannot go out unescorted."

"Of course not."

"I do have some manners," Mags insisted. "Please let her know that."

"I'll have to let her know more than that. Like that I love you."

"Will that be acceptable to her?"

Asa hesitated and she could see it in his eyes. "I'll make it so."

"I have never heard of a marriage beginning in such a way. Forget what I said in Georgia, Asa. It was in the heat of the moment when I was carried away. I'm sorry that I even said it."

"I'm not." He pushed back on the door.

"I am. Please leave."

"I will not, until I know that you aren't mad at me."

"I appreciate that you have brought me up here to a new life, but I'm trying to have my new life now and I appreciate it if you'll let me do that."

"Fine." Asa pushed the door open wider against her strength, and she stepped back. "But just know that you cannot shut me out. Ruby and Adam are my friends and I'll be calling regularly to see them."

"Which will probably not work out very well since Adam is busy with is work and Ruby is indisposed. Oh well."

"Then I'll be here to see you."

"And you'll have to ask Adam's permission to do that."

Adam and Solomon were running down the street. She let out a long breath. All would be revealed soon and she felt chagrined at knowing that her sister and brother-in-law would know just how foolish she had been. She was not looking forward to the revelation.

After all, she was the sensible one. Now, she was about to be shown up for who she really was, a lovesick crazed woman who had dared to propose to a man who didn't want her and who wasn't even strong enough to stand up to his mother to tell her that Mags was his own heart.

Why did these things always have to happen to her?

Chapter Nineteen

That proud tilt of her head made him want to kick himself. With the Bakelite leg.

He knew that he had messed up. Watching her go upstairs to her sister, he turned to Adam in front of the opened front door. “I’ve done it now.”

Adam clapped a hand on his shoulder and smiled. “When it comes to women, there is no predicting anything. What did you do?”

When he told him, Adam whistled and he felt a sinking feeling in his stomach. Yes, he had really made it worse with Mags. He didn’t like the thought of watching Mags become acclimated to Pittsburgh and then finding someone new to be her husband. Or worse yet, going back down to that terrible Southern town and being Winslow’s moneymaker plaything he could show off to his powerful friends. Mags deserved better than that. “You’ll have to show her you can be constant. Let her know that you are not going anywhere.”

“How am I to do that? She says she’s resolved to taking care of Ruby.”

Adam frowned. “I don’t like the sound of that. She’s not in prison up here.”

“You know how important it is to her to take care—it’s what she likes to do.”

“Yes, yes.” Adam frowned in thought. Solomon was making a lot of noise, Asa could see and the noise disturbed his father. “Go on upstairs to your aunt and mother,” Adam directed his son.

Solomon dragged his heels at his fun time being over, but he gave Asa a little wave and an idea occurred struck him. “If she’s taking care of Ruby, and you still have your patients and want to stay close to home to take care, what about Solomon?"

"We have the maid when she comes in, but I must confess, she's a little empty headed."

"That's the answer! I'll be Solomon's governess!"

Adam laughed. "We can't pay much, but you can have off on Sundays and every other Wednesday." He sobered. "Seriously, I know that you have more writing to do about the investigation. I can set you up at a desk here in the parlor. When the maid has Solomon, you can work, if you don't mind keeping him occupied."

"I don't."

"She needs to see you care."

"I do."

"I don't have a mother living, but I would know better than doing what you did."

"You know how Elodie can be."

"I know. And it'll all resolve itself if it is meant to," Adam said. Asa felt a sinking feeling again. He didn't like the vague nature of his friend's response. It had to work out. He couldn't afford to lose more in his life. He wouldn't.

A little later, Adam came up the stairs to the bedroom where Mags was seated on a chair next to her sister, reading a story. Solomon sat at her feet, entranced. "I'll wash up, my love and then I'll check on you," Adam said.

"Take your time, darling. Mags is reading to Solomon all about Greek mythology," Ruby informed him.

"I know that Mags has her hands full seeing to you, love, and so I've asked Asa to stay."

Mags turned around to look out Ruby's back window and surely, Asa lead his horse out to Adam's barn to stable it. "What do you mean, stay?"

"He's going to help with Solomon and work on his investigation notes."

Ruby clapped her hands. "An excellent idea."

"No it isn't," Mags said indignantly. "I can take care of everything. I don't need his help."

Ruby put her hand out on her sister's arm. "Everyone needs help from time to time."

"Finish the myth, Auntie."

"Let's go downstairs, and let your father see to your mother." She folded down the corner of the book page, closed the book and stood. "Call me when you are done."

"We surely will."

She walked out of the room with Solomon at her heels. Walking down the stairs, she could hear the sotto voice of her sister. "He loves her." Ruby never could whisper.

Then she couldn't hear Adam's response. She was too far down the stairs. Leave it to Ruby to try to engineer something with Asa. *Betrayal.* She took her nephew back into the parlor and heard the back door close. She and Solomon sat themselves on the davenport and waited for Asa to come in.

"What are you all doing back down here?"

"Auntie was reading me about the Titans, Mr. Caldwell," Solomon said.

"I would like to hear Auntie read too." Asa put his feet up on an ottoman, sitting in a big, winged chair.

"I'll read some more, but I cannot stay long. Once Adam has checked over Ruby, I'll have to go back upstairs." *And tell her off.*

"That's fine."

Mags actually finished the story, seething the whole time about the way these events were shaping her life. Relieved to hear Adam's footfall on the stairs, she stood, handing the book to Asa. "Here. I'm sure that Solomon would like to hear about how Zeus formed the earth and heavens."

"I would appreciate telling him. I have all the time in the world to make sure that he receives the proper attention." He took the book from her letting his hand cover hers and linger for much too long. She snatched her hand away, not caring at all for the intense look he gave her.

"That's interesting. It seems to me that when he needed attention earlier, you couldn't be bothered."

Asa went to stand, but she stopped him with a gesture. "That's not true, Mags I—"

"I have things to do."

"I want to explain."

"I want to hear another story, Mr. Caldwell," Solomon whined.

Adam stood in the doorway and seemed amused. "I had forgotten about how funny lovebirds can be."

"There aren't any birds in here, Daddy." Solomon seemed to be confused.

Adam smiled at his son. "After you are done reading your story, Mr. Caldwell and I will show you about playing checkers."

"I must get to my sister."

Asa grabbed her wrist. "I'll be here."

"Please let me go, Mr. Caldwell. Or whatever you call yourself. Enjoy reading your story."

"We will," Solomon piped in. "I like Mr. Caldwell, because he lets me knock on his leg to hear the echo inside."

"Solomon," Adam scolded. "Apologize."

There was a downturned frown on Solomon's adorable little face and Mags couldn't help but smile. So did Asa. "I'm sorry, Mr. Caldwell."

"That's okay, Solly. If I minded so very much, I wouldn't let you do it, would I? Now, where were we?"

He winked at her as she turned to leave. Appalling. Was there no end to this man's nerve? She walked briskly up the stairs to get back to Ruby and she saw her sister lying there in bed, protecting her distended belly with her hands. Mags's heart turned over. She didn't want to hurt her sister's feelings given her terrible restrictions and the worry she felt over the impending birth.

She knew that Ruby didn't understand and she was determined to make her sister see.

"Did you see Asa Caldwell?" her sister asked.

"He's down there."

"What did he say?"

Mags shrugged her shoulders as she returned to the chair next to Ruby, but Ruby patted the big space next to her and Mags settled in on the huge bed. The baby seemed to settle in for the news by moving the thin sheets on Ruby's stomach.

Please let her baby be okay. "What should he have said?"

Ruby clasped her sister's hands and put them next to her face and deepened her voice. "Please, please, darling Margaret. Come with me and be my love. We can be married in your sister's parlor right away and live in love."

"Right. That kind of thing doesn't happen for girls like me. That kind of thing happens for girls like you."

"What do you mean?"

Mags gestured all around her. "Mama and Daddy would be so proud to see how you live. Trust me, Ruby, it would only be you who would get swept up like a fairy princess to live in the great big castle. And you didn't even like fairy tales when we were growing up."

Ruby gave a wistful smile. "No, I never did. I never wanted to hear them. I knew that they weren't true for girls like us. So when you say, girls like me, what do you mean?"

"Of your beauty. The way that you look."

Ruby's eyebrows came together. "You're beautiful. You have the most magnificent skin and eyes."

"Skin?"

"Yes, your skin. Your skin is the most beautiful maple color and it glows so. I have these freckles that I've always disliked. I always wanted your skin."

Mags gave the wistful smile this time. "There are lots of others who don't like this skin."

"Who?"

"Elodie Caldwell," Mags choked out, feeling hurt at the mention of Asa's mother.

Ruby searched around in the room for a minute before a look of understanding dawned on her face. "I've thought something was wrong with you ever since you arrived. What's going on?"

"She was less than kind when she picked us up at the station."

"And?"

"And Asa did not defend me or say any of the things he said in Georgia."

"Like what?"

"Like that he loved me."

Ruby frowned. "He told you he loved you in Georgia? Did he kiss you?"

Lowering her head, she crossed her fingers together, too ashamed to answer. She knew Ruby understood.

When she looked up, Ruby had folded her arms as best as she could and pursed her lips together. "How was it?"

"Wonderful. I had always wondered if it would tickle if a man with face hair kissed me."

"And?"

"It doesn't. It feels," she struggled to find the word. "Exciting."

"Yes, it does." Ruby sat up a little bit more.

Mags reached over and helped her adjust her pillows. "Travis kissed like a little boy. Asa is a man, I had thought, until he backed down to his mother."

Ruby shook her head. "You aren't being fair. He hasn't backed down. He just hasn't stood up yet. That's what. He's standing up now. Trust me. Elodie is having a fit wondering why her son would want to be over here when he could be in that tomb of a house of hers, working on his writing. She knows. And she probably felt threatened by you. I don't think it was about your color."

She didn't want to repeat Elodie's nasty words. Besides, someone as light as Ruby could not know how she felt. Her sister's words made her feel a little bit better, though.

"And Asa was in a very dark place when he came back from the war. He had to adjust to his leg, and the loss of his...friend." Ruby swallowed.

"He loved her," Mags whispered.

"He loved her just as you loved Travis. It wasn't real love it was just new love. Everything that happened in Winslow tested you. This is another test, that's all. Elodie is harmless. When she sees what you can do…" Ruby rubbed her hands together. "You can take my place in organizing the fall bazaar. She'll lose her mind. You're just the kind of church worker she's been looking for."

"I couldn't believe it when Asa told me that you were doing that kind of church work."

Ruby waved a hand. "I have ideas. I don't make things come alive like you do. Trust me, you'll be embraced by the Caldwells. And by Asa."

"How do you know?"

"I can hear it in his voice when he talks to you."

"You can hear all the way up here?"

"Of course. When you have to stay in the bed all day long, your senses get perked up when they have nothing to do. I can hear him. Believe me, I intend to ask him what he is doing kissing my baby sister without offering to marry her—but he will."

"I don't want anyone's pity."

Ruby's face came together in a pucker. "I went to see him at his mother's before he left, about two months ago." Her sister had to gather herself, she could tell. "Do you remember how I was just after the attack?"

Mags remembered the dreadful spring and summer of 1914. Fruit budded out in their orchards, and things came alive, but not Ruby. Her sister Ruby stayed around the house all the time, a dead thing among them—the living. She nodded her head, almost as if the nodding could shake those bad memories from her brain.

"That's how he was. When I came to see him to ask him about the investigation, he was in bed. He had a pistol in his lap."

Mags put a hand to her mouth to stop the gasp. Her eyes shone with tears thinking of the amount of pain that would have caused Asa to take away one of God's greatest gifts—life. "What happened?"

Ruby shrugged her shoulders. "I went over to him and told him to give it to me."

"You have more nerve, Ruby. What did he do?"

"He seemed stunned by my request—this large bellied woman asking him for the pistol. I told him that I was a country girl and I knew guns. I took it and put it as far away from him as possible and told him that if he wanted to do away with himself, he would have to cross the room to do it. I said I had more important work for him to do."

"You saved his life. You and that nerve of yours," Mags whispered through her fingers.

Ruby touched her hand. "No love. You did that, my Margaret. I can hear it in his voice. And as soon as I'm able, whether it is proper or not, I'm going to have him up here. I want to see it on his face too."

Mags slid down and put her head on her shorter sister's shoulder. "I love him."

"I know you do. Part of why I sent him down there."

Mags sat up. "What?"

"He's up here, pining after some deceased foreign woman. I have four sisters, a couple of them ready for marriage. What do you think?" Ruby put her head on her shoulder again. "I always wanted a brother. I was tired of being the boy in the family."

"There's no denying it. You're insane."

"These things tend to be inherited. I know. I'm a nurse and I have studied these things." Ruby linked her fingers through hers. "If you marry him in say, two months, one month after I have the baby, so that I can come down and sit in the parlor and watch your wedding, do you realize that you could be me in a year's time?" She pointed to her stomach.

She drew back horrified and Ruby laughed at her.

"You always wanted to be a mother. You would be the best one of any of us."

"The rest of you sillies didn't even like playing with dolls. I usually forced Em and Delie to, because they were too young, but you and Nettie thought it was foolishness."

"I never liked the way that the dolls looked. They're creepy."

"And soon, you'll have your own doll." Mags put an affectionate hand on her sister's big belly.

"If you play your cards right, you can have yours too. They could be playmates for each other." Ruby jabbed her in the ribs with an elbow, making her laugh. Then she grew serious.

"We'll see."

"Do you doubt your big sister's ability to get involved in a lover's quarrel and make it all right?" Ruby put a thin arm around Mags's shoulders.

"No. I doubt that Asa is as resolved in his love as you say."

"We'll see, dear sister. We'll see."

Adam offered Asa the use of a guest room, and he stayed down the other end of the hall, for propriety's sake. Still, he dogged her steps from morning to night. So wearying.

In the protected circumstance of the Morson home, Asa could see that she was a crackerjack housewife, as he knew that she would be, and she knew he would be an amazing father. He took wonderful care of Solomon, and gave a great deal of relief to the household by keeping the energetic four-year-old occupied and distracted. He even started to teach him letters.

One day two weeks later, Asa went to make his report to Ruby. Before that, he had ducked his head inside to tell her good morning and good night, but had not really visited with her, lest she get upset over his report. Adam did not want anything to upset Ruby too much and Asa understood his protectiveness.

Mags made her sister a small bed jacket and put Ruby's hair up on top of her head. She climbed off of her usual perch in the bed next to her sister. She tried not to stare at him, or to be moved by his handsome good looks. It wasn't working.

"Well, well." Ruby's look at Asa brooked no nonsense. "Please. Have a seat and make your report."

"I presume that you've read my reports."

Ruby sobered. "I have. It's good that you went. It's even better you are back. Sounds like things are getting even worse."

"They are."

"And these reports will let other people know the horrors that have been going on. Thank you."

Asa nodded. "Thank you, ma'am. You look well."

"You lie well. But I appreciate it."

"In the horror, I found succor, and I want to thank you for that."

Ruby nodded rather formally. "Yes, I have heard. Do you intend to marry my sister?"

"If she'll have me."

"No," Mags did not hesitate. The two of them stared at her as if she were ready to be signed into the looney bin. "You're a very nice man. You play well with Solomon. You write wonderfully. I'm not going to marry where I'm not welcome."

Asa looked down at his hands. "I'll make her understand."

"People aren't made to understand. They just do as they will."

"She'll do as I will." Asa spoke so forcefully, that she almost jumped out of her skin. She composed herself, resolved not to let him or his pretty words get to her.

"Asa, please invite your mother to dinner tomorrow," Ruby offered.

"As you wish, ma'am." Asa nodded back at her.

"How'll you make that happen when you are in bed?" Mags demanded.

"I won't. You will."

"I don't think so."

Ruby fixed her sister with a sharp look. "It's my house. I feel that I have to consult with Elodie about the fall bazaar." She stroked her belly.

Mags felt a fist close over her heart, but she knew she owed her sister. "Fine. I'll do it."

"Thank you." Ruby leaned back on her pillows, appearing as a satisfied cat.

"And now, you should go home to your mother, since that's where you really belong," Mags put in.

"Mags! You should not speak to our guest in that way."

"I'm sorry, I did not mean to be rude, sister, only truthful."

"And Pearl knows how to be truthful with me." Asa looked amused at her outburst, instead of angry, which made her angrier.

"Pearl?" Ruby said looking between them.

"That's what I'm going to call her from now on. Mags doesn't suit her at all as far as I can see."

Mags walked out of the room with clenched fists. She was resolved to do as Ruby wanted and then she would make it clear—Asa had to go. But even as she thought it, she had a horribly empty feeling that things would be too, too quiet after he had gone.

Chapter Twenty

To do what Ruby wanted in less than one day took all of her organizing skills. If Mags knew how to curse, she would have, but then she felt bad, thinking of poor Ruby with her big stomach, and dark circles under her eyes waiting for her baby to come, praying for the baby to be healthy. Adam told her that this baby, when it came, would be Ruby's last.

Please forgive me, dear God. Look out for my sister and little one.

The dinner would be delicious, a beautiful roast with vegetables, a tall caramel cake and special summer peach tea. She woke early in the darkness, which in the summer was saying something, and began her day.

When she organized breakfast, she was chagrined to see Asa was already there with Solomon, planning on what to do for the day. At about three o'clock, he would take Solomon for a ride and go retrieve his mother for the meal.

The clock, then, became Mags's enemy. The house required a thorough going over cleaning-wise as well, because Ruby had been sick and had not been able to see to certain tasks for a long time. She and the maid worked hard, polishing furniture, beating rugs and polishing silverware. At about two o'clock, she went upstairs to take a bath inside of the bathroom, one of those luxuries that she could not get over, and dressed in her best white dress, piling her hair up on top of her head in a puffy cloud. At precisely four o'clock, she heard Asa make his way into the foyer with his mother, Solomon in tow.

When she finished her preparations and presented herself in front of her sister, Ruby told her, "Keep the door open so that I can hear."

"You owe me big," Mags muttered.

"You look just beautiful." Ruby clasped her hands.

"I appreciate the boost, but I don't want to do this."

"When you are finished with dinner, ask Elodie if she can come upstairs. Adam should be home soon, so I'll be all right."

"Call out if you aren't. And if not, then I can check on you. Or I can just stay up here."

"Get down there and do what you know how." Ruby waved her away as if she were a fly and inconsequential.

Mags grabbed a handful of her dress and alighted the stairs. She was glad that this dress had shorter sleeves ending at her elbow, so that she could be cool in this hot late-July day. Walking into the parlor, she was surprised to see that Solomon had finagled Elodie into reading him a story. Asa leaned on his cane to stand but she stilled him with a hand. She sat down on the chair opposite him, and watched as Elodie read to Solomon in a high-pitched voice, explaining all that Solomon wanted to know. As usual the explanations were extensive, because he was an inquisitive child.

When she was done, she sat back and folded the book over and gave Solomon a pleased look. "There you go, young man. What did you think?"

Solomon focused his devastating long-eyelashes look on the older woman. "You did okay, but Mr. Asa does horse voices when he reads it. Maybe if you had done that, it would have been better."

She wanted to take Solomon away quickly at her nephew's candor, but Elodie and Asa laughed. Elodie asked, "Well, who do you think taught him the horse voices, I would like to know?"

"The horses?"

They all laughed again and she joined in, despite her nerves. Elodie turned to her and nodded. "Miss Margaret. It's good to see you under some different circumstances."

"Yes. The train trip was a tiring event. I wasn't quite myself." There was a period of silence and Mags stood, smoothing her skirt. "I apologize on behalf of my sister and brother-in-law, but Adam is out on a call, and Ruby is indisposed."

Elodie's face took on worry. "I thought that she would be joining us."

"Given how stubborn she can be sometimes, she might have tried it, if she hadn't had problems before with her health." Mags put the situation in the delicate way that she knew an older woman would respond to.

"Yes. I see."

"She asked if you would come up after dessert. If you don't mind seeing her upstairs, that is."

"Highly irregular, but I haven't seen her in such a long time. I would like to lay eyes on her myself."

"Fine. If you're ready, the dinner table is set up for us in the dining room. Solomon will join us."

She could see her nephew's gray eyes light up. "Gee whillikers," he said.

"But he must behave."

She wanted to laugh at the downcast look on Solomon's face, but she kept her serious look as she guided them forward. Solomon took Elodie by the hand and escorted her into the dining room. The table was beautifully set and decorated with summer flower arrangements.

Asa arranged for his mother to sit in a chair on one side of the table and made sure that Solomon was placed upon enough cushions on the other side of the table nearest to himself and Mags.

"I'll serve," she announced.

"The maid isn't here?" Asa frowned.

"I sent her home. She worked earlier today than usual." *And harder.* She went into the kitchen donned a large duckcloth apron, and plated the roast and vegetables. The kitchen was hot, but she felt a cold trickle of sweat down her back as she lifted the steaming platter up and carried it through the door.

"Should I carve?" Asa stood with an eager look on his face.

Mags smiled at him. "If you wish."

"This is all very unusual," was all Elodie could say.

When Asa had served their plates, and said a rather sparse grace, they all began to eat in silence, except for small Solomon who was having a far easier time of it since Asa had cut his meat and vegetables.

"I love this meat! May I have some more, please?"

"I'm glad that you like it Solomon, but you need to eat your vegetables first." Mags cut into her own roast and sampled the meat along with some vegetables. *One of my best.*

"Your sister certainly sets a fine table," Elodie said, the first nice thing to come from her.

"Thank you," she said, not sure how to respond.

"Mother, as you know, Ruby has been on bedrest for almost a month. This is all Pearl's doing. It's wonderful, my love."

Later, upon reflection of the moment, she would laugh at the way Elodie's head snapped around at the endearments Asa had put into his compliment, but at the time, it made her warm all over. "Thank you."

"Asa, I didn't know that you were in the habit of speaking to young, unmarried women in such a fashion," Elodie spoke around her food as she ate more of her dinner—which Mags noticed she had been doing nonstop since got her plate and grace was said.

Asa gazed at her, his heart in his eyes this time. A thrill of joy went up her arms and she swallowed, pleased at his scrutiny, but somewhat chagrined at this close attention in front of his mother. "I'm in the habit of speaking that way to my fiancée. Pearl, will you be my wife?"

Mags felt a little thrill as he said it and a bubble of delight worked its way up her throat and unintentionally come out of her mouth. She could see that Elodie viewed her as if she had two heads, but she couldn't help it. "I'm so glad that you like the roast, Mr. Caldwell, but you don't have to propose to me about it."

"Well," Elodie said, pausing to lift her plate for more, "I'm glad to see that someone around here has some manners."

Asa laughed at what she said. "Pearl. It's just that good. As are you." He turned serious all of a sudden. "You're worth it."

"If you marries him," Solomon piped up, "then Mr. Caldwell can be my uncle and Mrs. Caldwell can be my, hmm."

Mags could see Elodie fixing him with a look of love and thought that she was a compassionate woman towards children, so she couldn't be all bad. Maybe it might be okay, if she were to marry Asa. "I would be your great friend, Solly, as

I always have been. But we would be family." Elodie looked around. "Everything here is beautiful. You're responsible for all of this?"

"Yes, ma'am."

Elodie had started to cut into the meat again and laid it down. "I wouldn't be disloyal to my friend Ruby for anything, but she isn't much of a housekeeper. If you turned this house around from what it was, speaks volumes for your skills. I have never seen it look this way before. I've had dinner here in the past, but the food has never been this delicious before."

"It's all Pearl, mother. She helped her mother with boarders in their home in the South. I'm firmly convinced she can do anything." Asa's eyes sparkled at her.

"Thank you."

"I didn't know you when you first arrived, Miss Margaret, but I have to admit, you are a wonder to have turned your sister's circumstances around. You are to be congratulated. If you're what Asa wants, then…" Elodie picked up her fork and knife and ate some more of her meat, "…God's blessings on you. Get him out of the house. He's getting on to thirty, for goodness sake."

Asa stood, and Mags did as well, in spite of herself. She came to him and they embraced. Right in front of his mother, he kissed her, but quickly on her lips with a peck, not lingering as he had done before. She wanted to melt away, but when she looked back at Elodie, she was eating. Solomon had slipped away declaring that he was going to tell his mother.

"I love you, my Pearl," Asa declared, not caring anymore if Elodie heard.

"I love you, Asa."

"So glad we've got that settled. No more Winslow for you. You're never to go back to Winslow, ever."

"Whatever you say." Mags sighed with happiness as she put her head on his shoulder.

"That was wonderful." Elodie wiped her mouth with her napkin. "What's for dessert?"

"She made one of her layer cakes, Mother."

"Caramel."

Elodie clasped her hands and gazed at Mags with, she thought for the first time, fondness. "Would you like to work our fall bazaar? Ruby will still be recuperating with the baby and we need someone with your talents there."

"I would love to." She nodded her head. "Let me get the coffee started for the cake."

"Yes indeed," Elodie declared.

Mags hummed a bit more as went into the kitchen and started organizing the coffee pot when she heard Solomon's fast footfall into the dining room and his piping voice sounded alarmed. She went to the kitchen door and looked out. Both Asa and his mother looked up at her. Elodie spoke. "Solomon says his mother is making some funny noises in her bed."

She had never run so fast up the stairs before. When she emerged in the doorway, she saw her sister lying on the bed, grasping at the sheets. Ruby's face was red with embarrassment. "I wet the bed. The baby is coming, Mags. I need help."

"I'm here." She stepped forward on shaky legs. She wasn't a nurse. That was Ruby.

"Where's Adam?"

She searched her mind, in complete and sheer panic. "He's on a call."

"He could be anywhere." Ruby's eyes were panicked and large. "I'm scared."

To her astonishment, Elodie came into Ruby's room, rolling up her sleeves, donning another duck cloth apron. "Fine way to get me up here to discuss the fall bazaar, Ruby. I've sent Asa and Solomon off in the carriage to find your husband. We'll have to make do ourselves here, miss." Elodie's look down at Ruby was filled with love and affection. Was it possible that Mags had misjudged this woman?

Tears, not sweat, ran down Ruby's face. This was Ruby, the powerhouse sister who organized lynching drives and created unions out of nothing. "I'm scared. If I lose this one, I want Adam to be here."

Elodie grasped Ruby's hand and used her other to grasp Mags's hand. "We're going to pray." Mags fell to her knees along with Elodie. "Dear God, we need you in this room today. We need you to give strength to our beloved sister

Ruby, who has had a hard time of it God. We need you to be here by her side, God. Give her strength at this time and be with her and this new life she is trying to bring into the world. Help her, Lord. In your name, Amen."

"Amen," Mags answered, stunned at the tears on her own face.

"Amen," Ruby whispered and Elodie pulled her sheets down and she quailed to see sister's propped up thin legs against her impossibly huge stomach and that the bedsheets were completely wet.

"Please wash your hands and arms," Ruby said.

Mags and Elodie went into the bathroom and washed thoroughly. "What if Adam doesn't get here?"

"We'll have to bring the baby ourselves," Elodie said. "I have had five children and Ruby is a nurse. I have to believe that'll be enough until Asa finds him and he comes."

"I see."

"You aren't squeamish are you, Miss Margaret?" Elodie demanded.

"I can do this." Mags swallowed, but stiffened her spine. She would do anything to help her sister.

"Wonderful." Elodie's face carried a new respect for her. "Let's go."

Gratefully, Mags took her turn at the washbowl after seeing Elodie march into the room. *Please, please let Adam come. Let him come.*

He didn't come.

Reflecting back on it, she knew that the birth of Ruby's daughter was the closest glimpse she would get into the face of God. Her heart cried out for joy when, just an hour later, the long, skinny body of Ruby's daughter slid into her hands. The little girl squalled and cried. Elodie came forward and cut the cord, bringing clean linen to keep the baby warm, taking her into the washroom.

"Is she okay?" Ruby sat up, understandably dazed at what had just happened having lost blood and some of the life forces.

"She's fine," Elodie called out. "She's as beautiful as her mother, with a head full of black hair and as white as a cotton ball."

She wanted to step in the bathroom to get the baby herself, but Elodie came forward with the squalling baby swaddled in her arms and handed her to

Ruby. Ruby's face transformed. "Oh. Oh, she's beautiful. Mags, she looks like Solomon."

"She does." She tried not to sniff as she viewed the wonder of her little niece.

The light that shone from her sister's eyes seemed to calm the baby. She knew who her mother was. "I love her so much, already. I was afraid that, when she came, she would be all blue like the others, but look at her. She's beautiful."

"She is." Elodie attended to her sister, and Mags wiped her own face, gathering up soaked linen to take down to the wash closet. "A little miracle."

"What will you call her?" When Mags returned to the room, Elodie had some waste to dispose of and she left. "I told Paul Winslow that you were going to have a girl and that you would call her Mary Margaret."

"You did not!" Ruby declared. "That was naughty of you."

"It served my purpose at the time," Mags said.

"I should really ask Adam." Ruby sniffed. "But he's on a call and I'll remind him of that whenever he asks me about her name. I'm going to name her Margaret Elodie. We'll call her Maisie."

Mags put a hand up to her cheek, feeling that it was growing warm. "I'm so flattered, Ruby."

"So you were half right."

Elodie came back in and seemed more emotional at hearing the little girl's name. "I am too, Ruby Jean. Thank you, honey."

"It's fitting that you are a part of her life since you're going to be in the family now."

They stood there silent for a minute, but then Mags thought about something. "How did you know that I was engaged?"

Ruby looked up at her for just a second, and her eyes were smiling. "I always knew, from the moment I sent Asa down there to you. You just had to figure it out."

Her sister's words confused her as she heard the door slam and Adam's hurried footfall up the stairs. He emerged through the door with a worried expression on his face.

"She's fine," Mags said to the mustachioed blur that passed her by to the washstand first, wanting to know all, right away.

"Leave it to you, Ruby to not even wait for the doctor." Adam scrubbed and chuckled, clearly happy, "But she is so lovely, honey and she's the picture of health. I can see that from here."

Ruby's face shone with pride, making both Mags and Elodie teary as Ruby presented Maisie to her father. They both left, taking off their aprons for the linen closet, going down the stairs to meet Asa and Solomon sitting in the parlor.

"You have a new sister," she told Solomon.

"Oh no."

"Oh yes." Mags sat on the other side of him and held his little hand. "And we are grateful to God for her life."

"We are," Asa intoned. "We are grateful to him for many things."

"We are."

"When can we be married in this parlor?" Asa asked her. "I think that Solomon's sister...does she have a name?"

"Margaret Elodie. Maisie."

"Maisie would like a playmate cousin close to her age."

Mags lowered her head. "Well, I can probably pull a wedding in a few weeks' time. A month or so. Something like a cousin for Solomon would take longer."

So on a late August day, three days after her twenty-first birthday, wearing a brand new string of pearls her husband bought for her, they were married in Ruby's parlor with Ruby, Adam, Solomon, Elodie and Asa's sisters and family looking on with pride and love. Maisie slept through it all.

Surrounded by love on that special day, Mags knew that she had come to this time and place through God's grace, manifest in precious nature of the necklace she wore—a true sign of her husband's love and devotion to her and for her.

Author's Note

The summer of 1919 was not just one of turmoil for Asa and Mags. Asa represents the population of The Great War who were not at all satisfied to be complacent after they had fought for the United States. Glenda Gilmore's *Defying Dixie: The Radical Roots of Civil Rights 1919-1915* clearly traces the Civil Rights Movement to before Montgomery and Rosa Parks. When they returned home, soldiers felt they had a right to demand better lives.

The result of these demands during the "Red" Summer of 1919 was an increase in lynching—killing outside of the law by any means necessary. When someone like John Bledsoe spoke about lynching, he was not referring to a method of killing by vigilante mob, like hanging. He was referring to all of the ways in which African Americans were confronted with the threat of violence. Thus, people could be lynched by several methods—and were. These incidents were regularly reported in newspapers like *The Chicago Defender* and *The Pittsburgh Courier*. Journalists like Asa, were sent to report on these horrors. Their reporting lead to the renewed vigor of The Great Migration when people like Mags began to steal themselves away with increased frequency. The leave-taking from the South by millions of African Americans was a direct reaction to forces of oppression and violence.

To learn more about the history surrounding Mags and Asa:

Cobb, Charles. This Nonviolent Stuff'll Get You Killed

Epstein, Abraham. The Negro Migrant in Pittsburgh

Foley, Barbara. Spectres of 1919

Lee, Chana Kai. For Freedom's Sake: The Life of Fannie Lou Hamer (all

about a great female manager)
McWhirter, Cameron. Red Summer
Wilkerson, Isabel. The Warmth of Other Suns: The Epic Story of America's Great Migration

About the Author

Piper Huguley, named the 2015 Debut Author of the year by Romance Slam Jam, Breakout Author of 2015 by the AAMBC and a top ten historical romance author in Publisher's Weekly by Beverly Jenkins, is a two-time Golden Heart® finalist. She is the author of "Migrations of the Heart," a five-book series of historical romances set in the early 20th century featuring African American characters. Book one in the series, *A Virtuous Ruby*, won the Golden Rose contest in Historical Romance in 2013 and was a Golden Heart® finalist in 2014. Book four, *A Champion's Heart*, was a Golden Heart® finalist in 2013.

Huguley is also the author of the "Home to Milford College" series. The series follows the building of a college from its founding in 1866. On release, the prequel novella to the "Home to Milford College" series, *The Lawyer's Luck*, reached #1 Amazon Bestseller status on the African American Christian Fiction charts.

Piper blogs about the history behind her novels at www.piperhuguley.com. She lives in Atlanta, Georgia with her husband and son.

A sheikh without a country. A woman without fear. A love hotter than the Sahara.

Mirage

© 2007 Monica Burns

In his heart, Viscount Blakeney will always be Sheikh Altair Mazir, but a deathbed oath to his English grandfather forces him to divide his time between Britain and his beautiful Sahara. A victim of prejudice from both cultures, he has learned to trust no one.

Yet when he witnesses firsthand the British Museum's rejection of Alexandra Talbot's request for assistance in finding the lost city of Ramesses II, he finds himself not only compelled to help, but donning his desert robes to hide his identity.

Alexandra is all too familiar with men who equate her sex with a lack of intelligence. But the mysterious Altair isn't like other men. He never questions her ability to find the lost city, only her resistance to the sinful pleasure of his touch.

Bound by a Pharaoh's prophecy, desire flares between them under the desert stars. But murder and betrayal turn their quest into a deadly game, pushing their fragile trust to the breaking point. A trust that must be reforged if they are to survive.

Warning: Contains a half-blood prince of the desert whose tortured Bedouin heart beats beneath a proper English cravat. And an American archaeologist who'll go a long way to fulfill her dreams.

Never steal a heart unless you can afford to lose your own.

True Pretenses
© 2015 Rose Lerner

Through sheer force of will, Ash Cohen raised himself and his younger brother from the London slums to become the best of confidence men. He's heartbroken to learn Rafe wants out of the life but determined to grant his brother his wish.

It seems simple: find a lonely, wealthy woman. If he can get her to fall in love with Rafe, his brother will be set. There's just one problem—Ash can't take his eyes off her.

Heiress Lydia Reeve is drawn to the kind, unassuming stranger who asks to tour her family's portrait gallery. And if she married, she could use the money from her dowry for her philanthropic schemes. The attraction seems mutual and serendipitous—until she realizes Ash is determined to matchmake for his younger brother.

When Lydia's passionate kiss puts Rafe's future at risk, Ash is forced to reveal a terrible family secret. Rafe disappears and Lydia asks Ash to marry her. Leaving Ash to wonder—did he choose the perfect woman for his brother, or for himself?

Warning: Contains secrets and pies.

She played right into his hands.

Her Wicked Captain

© 2014 Sandra Jones

Possessing uncanny people-reading skills like her mama, Philadelphia "Dell" Samuels has spent thirteen years in her aunt's rustic Ozarks home, telling fortunes over cards and trying to pass as white. But the treacherous Mississippi River childhood her mama dragged her away from catches up to her on a steamboat captained by her old friend Rory Campbell.

Rory is a gambler in need of a miracle. Following the cold trail of his boss's wife and bastard daughter, Dell, Rory has only one goal in mind: saving his crew from the boss's cruelty by ruining him. He's convinced he can lure his boss into a high-stakes game against a rival, and with Dell's people-reading skills, the monster will lose everything.

Under Rory's tutelage and protection, Dell agrees to the tortured captain's plan. Passion and peril bring them together as lovers. But when the plan goes awry, the lives of the innocent depend on Dell's ability to read the situation correctly—and hopefully save them all.

Warning: There's not enough moonshine on the Mississippi to keep this fortuneteller from saving The Devil's Henchman, a high-stakes gambler—and her childhood friend—from his boss's cruel attentions. Touches upon issues of child abuse, revenge, and redemption.

CPSIA information can be obtained at www.ICGtesting.com
Printed in the USA
LVOW07s1728121016

508485LV00004B/779/P